SUPERB WRITING
TO FIRE THE IMAGINATION

Celia Rees writes: I am interested in the way that the past underlies the present; how perfectly ordinary places, otherwise hardly worth a second glance, are shadowed by sinister events from the past. Many of our ancient cities host ghost walks which invite us to visit such places and it was on just such a walk that I had the idea for this series. I found myself thinking: What if there were two cities? The one we live in – and one that ghosts inhabit. What if at certain times of the year and in certain places, the barriers between the two worlds grow thin, making it possible to move from one to the other? And if ghosts lived there, why not others? Creatures we know from myth and legend, creatures so powerful that even the ghosts fear them? Just a story? Maybe. But on a recent visit to that city, I found that several of the ghost walk routes had been abandoned, because of poltergeist activity . . .

Celia Rees has written many books for children and teenagers and enjoys writing in different genres. She hopes what interests her will interest other people, be it ghosts, vampires, UFOs or witch trials. Her latest books, *Truth or Dare* and *Witch Child*, have been published to critical acclaim.

*Other titles available from Hodder Children's Books:*

The Brugan
Dead Edward
*Stephen Moore*

Daughter of Storms
The Dark Caller
Keepers of Light
Mirror Mirror 1: Breaking Through
Mirror Mirror 2: Running Free
Mirror Mirror 3: Testing Limits
*Louise Cooper*

Owl Light
Night People
Alien Dawn
*Maggie Pearson*

Power to Burn
*Anna Fienberg*

The Lammas Field
*Catherine Fisher*

The Law of the Wolf Tower
Queen of the Wolves
*Tanith Lee*

The Boxes
*William Sleator*

# A Trap in Time

## CELIA REES

*Hodder*
*Children's*
*Books*

a division of Hodder Headline Limited

*For Jacob,*
*and for Peter*

First published as separate volumes:
*U is for Unbeliever* and *N is for Nightmare* in 1998
by Hodder Children's Books

This bind-up edition published in 2002
by Hodder Children's Books Limited

10 9 8 7 6 5 4 3 2 1

A Catalogue record for this book
is available from the British Library

ISBN 0 340 81801 8

Typeset by Hewer Text Ltd, Edinburgh
Printed and bound in Great Britain by
Clays Ltd, St Ives plc

Hodder Children's Books
A Division of Hodder Headline Limited
338 Euston Road
London NW1 3BH

# Christmas

# A Trap in Time

All through the city and its suburbs, the past lies behind the present and ghosts shadow the living. There are threshold zones, borderlines, and places where the laws of time and space falter. Strange things can happen, the barriers between the worlds grow thin and it is possible, just possible, to move from one world to another . . .

For Davey Williams, his sister and cousins, a desperate race is now on. Davey must act quickly if he is to escape the deadly trap that has been set for him; and they must work together if they are to prevent an all-out war between the living and the dead.

Davey Williams had plenty of reasons to believe in ghosts
and ghouls. He knew that they existed because he had met
some. He knew their haunts. He knew that some were
good and some were bad; some were beyond even that.
Davey had become used to the idea of a world alongside
ours, peopled by ghosts with parallel lives. He had even
come to accept that sometimes it was possible to slip in
between time and end up on the wrong side. He just had
not thought that such things would happen on a school
trip.

In fact nothing was further from his mind as he shuffled
along with the other pupils, getting ready to view the next
exhibit in the local museum. They were spending the day
here. It was getting near to Christmas and the visit was a
combined end–of–term treat and a fitting finish to their
History project on Life in Victorian England.

'This is not, of course, one of our best examples . . .'
The guide smirked as she indicated the sampler on the
wall.

They had already seen the Parlour, Kitchen and School,
now it was the Nursery. When it came to his turn, Davey
stood well back from the ropes that separated the little
room from the rest of the world. His class had already

been warned about setting off alarms by getting too close to the exhibits. He glanced up at the piece of needlework that the guide had singled out for scorn. Cross-stitched letters of the alphabet stood above a little grey house. To the side of that was a big tree which looked a bit like a yellow umbrella. Along the bottom was a row of spidery flowers, in the middle, the initials: E*A*H. There were a few odd-shaped stitches, and one or two of the letters might have slipped a bit, but it looked all right to him. It was better than anything he could do.

Davey lingered for a moment to look at the rest of the room. Besides the sampler, the walls held other pictures: figures from rhymes and cautionary tales, Jack and Jill going up the hill, Straw-headed Peter with his standing shock of hair and horrible dagger nailed fingers. A bunch of dolls sat propped up along a white counterpaned bed. China-faced, cupid-lipped, with spiky hands and booted feet, they leaned against a group of teddies. Some of these were nearly bald; others, long-nosed and thin, had straggly whiskers which made them look like little old men. A couple of painted wooden soldiers stood at each end of the row, as if on guard. The whole lot of them had been lined up to face a miniature blackboard. Davey smiled. He used to do that, play school with his toys, give them a really hard time. His little sister, Emma, still did. You could sometimes hear her shouting at them. Davey was just thinking about that, about how little things changed, when:

*Weeooh, Weeooh, Weeooh!*

Somewhere near to him a loud electronic wailing began. He nearly jumped out of his skin.

There was a moment of shocked silence. The lady guiding them round sniffed hard and then looked disgusted, as if she'd breathed in a bad smell. The rest of his class were cracking up as Mr Craddock came pushing through from the back shouting:

'Who did that? Who did that?'

They were all dressed up in various ways meant to approximate Victorian days. Davey himself was wearing a kind of sailorsuit bib thing over an old jacket and a pair of his dad's trousers, cut down to fit him. Craddock had his hair parted in the middle and plastered down. He was wearing his scary Jekyll and Hyde outfit, last seen at Hallowe'en. He had been in a good mood then, now he was more Mr Hyde as he came striding towards Davey.

'Davey Williams. I might have known . . .'

'I didn't do it. I didn't go anywhere near it. Honest, Sir . . .'

'How many times do you have to be told! Do not touch! Do not go near the barrier!' He stared down at Davey, upper lip curling, black brows frowning. 'How old are you? Eleven? Twelve? I might as well be in charge of a group of five-year-olds!'

'But Sir! I didn't—'

The teacher held up his hand for silence. Davey let his own words fade into Craddock's tirade. He had been standing at least a metre away from the barrier. He could not have possibly set it off, but the teacher had already made up his mind, so arguing was pointless.

Craddock was really going for it now. Davey looked round. The guide was smirking at him and all his classmates were killing themselves; loving every minute, falling about, relieved it wasn't them being singled out. Davey stared at the ground, his cheeks stinging with all the laughter directed at him.

There was one strange thing, though. One odd thing. One laugh had begun before the rest, straight after the alarm went off. He had heard it clearly, a low musical chuckle, trilling behind the electronic wailing sound, and it had come from inside the nursery room, on the other side of the barrier.

It was not until he went outside at lunchtime that he began to work it out.

The day was warm for early December. The heating was working overtime. The room set aside for school parties was stuffy and full. Some of the lads had already sloped out, looking for a game of football. Davey followed them into the garden, thinking to eat his lunch out there and then maybe have a kick about.

He walked around the little sunken lawn, where the *Keep Off the Grass* notices were being ignored, heading towards a paved area set about with wooden benches. People from the other class occupied these benches, there was only one free. It was under a very large tree, a weeping willow, rather like the one in the sampler, which drooped over that whole corner of the garden.

Although winter had stripped its leaves, long thin whippy fronds hung down, thick as a curtain. Davey parted these and walked in, only to notice, just at the last minute, that there was someone else sitting there. A girl. Davey thought at first glance that she must be from the other class. They were not the only ones on the visit, 7JM were there as well. Davey knew them, of course, but maybe this girl was new to the school and had only just joined them. Whatever the case, he had to admire her outfit. She could have stepped out of one of the glass cases that they had paraded past in the Costume section. Her clothes looked accurate down to the very last detail, as though she had hired them from a shop.

'Oh, I'm sorry,' he said, preparing to back out. 'I didn't see you . . .'

'That's all right.' She looked up at him and smiled.

Davey moved closer. She seemed familiar. Davey looked into her grey eyes, set wide apart in a pale heart-shaped face.

'Are you in Miss Malkin's class?' he asked.

'No,' she said and laughed, shaking out her long wavy dark hair. 'I've been waiting for you, Davey.'

It was the laugh which gave her away, high and silvery. Davey felt the goosebumps rise all up his arms. At the same time his insides seemed to sink, as if he was in a lift that was descending too fast.

'Elizabeth?' he asked, groping for the side of the bench. He had to sit down.

'Yes,' she laughed again. 'Do you remember now?'

He had met Elizabeth on that strange evening last midsummer. She was a ghost. She lived at an inn called *The Seven Dials* along with Jack Cade, the highwayman, and Polly and Govan. She had shown Davey how to haunt; they had shared adventures together. Davey had not seen her since that night when he had left the ghost city. Now here she was, in the middle of *his* world, sitting at a picnic table, as though it was the kind of thing she did every day.

'How did you get here?' he managed to ask, despite the tightness gripping his throat.

'They have some things of mine in the museum. This dress,' she smoothed the green grey silk, 'some toys in the Nursery and a piece of my embroidery.'

'E★A★H – that's you isn't it?' Davey asked, realisation suddenly dawning on him. 'You were there this morning. You set the alarm off. I heard you laughing.'

'Yes.' She smiled. 'Elizabeth Ann Hamilton. That was me. After I died, my mother kept my things, she could not bear to part with them, I suppose. Much later they were donated to this place. I often set off the alarm to annoy Mrs Summers.'

'Mrs Summers?' Davey frowned.

'The guide. She points out the faults in my needlework and I consider that most unkind. I was only nine at the time.'

'What are you doing here now? I thought you had to stay in the city?'

'You do not know all the rules of haunting. My belongings are here. That allows me in. I've been waiting for you.'

'Since when?'

'Oh, a while.'

Ghosts were extremely vague about time because it did not really exist for them in any normal sense. Davey was curious about that. He still did not understand how they filled the yawning gaps. What did they do?

'I haunt some of the rooms,' she said, in answer to his unspoken question. 'Particularly those Mrs Summers oversees.' She shrugged. 'Other than that I play cards with the soldiers. There's practically a whole regiment up in the military section. They are having some kind of reunion.' Somewhere behind them a handbell sounded. 'But this visit has a purpose.' Elizabeth was suddenly serious. 'I am here to warn you. We cannot waste time in idle chit-chat.'

'Warn me? What about?'

'I have been sent by the Blind Fiddler. Do you remember him?'

Davey nodded. The old man was as clear in his mind as if he was standing right there with them: cloaked in black, wearing a broad-brimmed hat, carrying a violin. Davey could see his craggy lined face, his smile, wise and kind, his blind eyes bulging like marbles, showing blue-white. The Blind Fiddler had saved them, got them out of the ghost city. Not just Davey but his sister, Kate, and his cousins, Tom and Elinor.

'The old man cannot see with his eyes,' Elizabeth was saying, 'but his hearing is as good as ever. He knows the business of the city better than any other. He says to tell you to expect trouble.'

'Why?'

'It has to do with the Old Grey Man's daughter and that little boy she took.'

Davey stared, eyes wide. Even to think of *her* gave him the shivers.

'I thought that what happened at Hallowe'en, with Jack and the Guytrash – I thought that had her sorted . . .'

'Had her sorted?' Elizabeth's eyebrows quirked at the unfamiliar phrase. 'Apparently not. You have thwarted her twice now, piling insult on insult. You know her kind are unforgiving. The enmity between you runs deep.'

Davey nodded miserably, his heart sinking inside him. He had thought to be rid of the fear he was feeling. The Old Grey Man's daughter was Other, neither human nor ghost. Her father was leader of the Host, the Sidhe, the Unseelie Court. They were fairies, but like nothing he had encountered in stories. At midsummer, Davey had saved a child from her, a human boy, stolen to be her toy.

At Hallowe'en, she had come after him. Davey shivered again, the day growing cold around him. Suddenly he could feel her presence, her malevolence . . .

'Davey!' Davey turned at the sound of his name being called. 'Davey? Is that you under here?' The willow curtain parted and Lisa Wilson, a friend from his class, came through the branches. 'I've been searching for you everywhere.' She peered about curiously. 'Who were you talking to?'

Davey glanced quickly behind him. Elizabeth had disappeared.

'Nobody.' He shrugged, trying not to look shifty. 'I'm on my own here.'

'Oh.' Lisa stared down at him, arms folded. 'I thought I saw a girl. Grey dress, long dark hair?'

'No.' Davey shook his head, quick to deny it. 'I've been on my own the whole time.'

'Must be my mistake.' She looked round again, not quite convinced. 'I could have sworn there was someone else in here . . . You ought to watch that,' she added, giving him a sharp look.

'Watch what?'

'Talking to yourself,' Lisa grinned. 'First sign of madness.'

'Oh, yeah. Right.' Davey laughed with nervous relief. Lisa was the most down-to-earth practical person he knew. She did not even read her horoscope, let alone believe in the supernatural. He would have had a hard time telling her that he had been talking to a ghost.

'Come on.' Lisa turned to make her way back. 'The rest have gone in. That's what I came to say. We'll be late if we're not careful.'

Davey followed her through the willow curtain, thinking about his lucky escape, glad that he didn't have to explain about Elizabeth. It did not occur to him until some time later how strange it was that Lisa had actually seen the ghost girl.

# 2

They were late. Ordinarily this would not have mattered very much, but this afternoon, lessons were to be conducted in the museum's schoolroom. The pupils sat in uniform rows, all squashed together, clamped behind long wooden desks. It was their class's turn to take part in the *Victorian Classroom Experience*.

There was none of the usual pre-registration chatter. Davey and Lisa were met with stony silence. Thirty pairs of eyes turned to stare and then turned back to Mr Craddock. The teacher was standing on a raised platform at the front of the room, towering over them. He held a long thin cane which he swished up and down and he seemed to have the entire class brainwashed. He wasn't allowed to hit anybody, but they were all watching the motion of his hand like mesmerised rabbits.

'Ah, David Williams, Elizabeth Wilson.' The cane whistled through the air. 'Nice of you to join us.'

Davey and Lisa stared at each other, their full names made them feel like strangers. They looked round the classroom. Neither could see a place to sit. Lisa's eyes scanned the room, every bench was full. Lisa's friend, Heidi, shuffled up for her, but Davey couldn't see a place.

'Sit down,' Mr Craddock barked at him. 'Stop dithering about!'

'But, Sir, there isn't anywhere.'

'There's a place right here, Davey. What's the matter with you?'

Davey looked down. For a second he seemed to see Elizabeth's grey eyes laughing up at him, and then he was staring at an empty space.

'Now, can we start?'

Mr Craddock rolled his eyes to the ceiling before resuming his slow pace up and down.

'As I was saying before I was so rudely interrupted, life was different in Victorian classrooms, very different. We had these for a start.'

The cane whistled through the air, its tip inches from the noses in the front row.

'It was quite legal and no Victorian schoolmaster would hesitate to use it.' The cane whipped back again. 'Do you hear me?'

People nodded, he had their full attention.

'I have other devices here designed to help the teacher in his job, sadly they are no longer available.' He paused but nobody laughed, the class weren't sure if he was joking or not. 'This, for example,' he held up a strange yoke-like contraption, 'was strapped to the back of anyone who slouched and slumped about. So *sit up straight*!' The whole class jolted upright. 'And this should need no introduction.'

He held up a large cardboard cone with DUNCE printed

on the side and it seemed to Davey that the teacher was looking straight at him.

'Some people will have worn this before the afternoon's out,' he added with a grin. 'That's if I'm not mistaken. Now. Pay attention.'

He put the dunce's cap down and turned to the chalk board. This was not like the boards at school. It stood on its own, not fixed to the wall, and was ruled like paper. Mr Craddock began writing the alphabet, sloping and curling the letters above and below the lines.

'You will find a slate on the desk in front of you and a special pencil,' he said without turning round. 'This is what Victorian children used in class. I want you to use it now to copy this down . . .'

The slate was divided up like the board. Davey picked up the pencil. It felt thin and slippery in his fingers, hard to grasp. His handwriting was not exactly the best in the class. The letters he made now wobbled all over the place. They looked nothing like Craddock's neat looping strokes. He could not even get them pointing in the same direction. Davey was aware of the teacher prowling up and down the rows. He had never known the class so quiet, you could have heard a pin drop. Craddock was pretty strict, but not like this. He was really acting the part of a Victorian schoolmaster.

Davey wrote the letters: *abcd*

Then something else began to appear. A message in immaculate copperplate:

Davey looked up sharply, checking for Craddock's whereabouts. Miss Malkin was the new teacher. She was here in the museum with the other class. Craddock fancied her. He chatted her up at every opportunity. If he saw this he would go absolutely mental. Davey stared, eyes wide, as more letters formed.

*She is not what she seems*

The teacher's footsteps were creaking near. Sweat broke out all across Davey's upper lip.

*She is*

Davey did not dare look at what the last word was. He let out a small whinnying sound and covered the lot with his hand, just as the cane came crashing down on the desk next to him. Craddock might be acting, but he certainly enjoyed waving that stick about.

'What are you doing, boy?'

Davey looked up into the teacher's brown eyes.

'N – nothing, Sir,' he stammered. 'I – I –'

'You were writing with your left hand,' the teacher barked back at him.

'Yes, Sir.' Davey grinned, relieved. 'It's the one I always use.'

'In Victorian times, it would have been tied behind your back. You would have worn the dunce's cap until you learnt to use your right.'

'Hey, Sir, that's bit harsh.' Davey laughed nervously, thinking Craddock must be joking. He was in danger of taking his Victorian schoolmaster part a little too far.

The teacher ignored him. 'Let's have a look at your efforts.'

Davey moved his hand slowly, afraid to show his slate. Much to his relief, the message had disappeared, only his own small crooked letters remained.

'Terrible.' Craddock curled his lip. 'Out to the front of the class. You'll have to do better than that on the board or that cap has got *your* name on it.'

'But, Sir,' Davey protested. 'That's not fair!'

'In Victorian times, there was no answering back.' Mr Craddock swished the cane about. 'You would have had a dose of that. Now, do as I say and look smart about it! Copy the top line.'

Davey sighed and got up from his place. The rest of the class were sniggering quietly, glad it wasn't them again. They all knew he was rubbish at handwriting and were happily anticipating his humiliation. Davey picked up the chalk. Craddock had no right to do this. He was going way over the top . . .

Suddenly Davey felt a light touch on his hand. He turned slightly. No one was there, but Elizabeth's voice breathed in his ear.

'It's easy,' she said. 'Let me guide you.'

The chalk flowed across the board and letters formed in writing far more perfect and elegant than Craddock's efforts.

'I must speak with you at length,' Elizabeth whispered

15

as they wrote. 'But it is dangerous for me now and there is so little time. Can you be here tomorrow? It is quiet in the morning.'

Davey nodded. The next day was Saturday.

'Very well. I will watch for you. Look for me in the room by the stairs. I . . .'

Davey was nearly at the end of the letters when his hand stopped on the board. Elizabeth had gone from his side. He was alone again.

No one in the class noticed anything. They had been distracted by the door opening.

'Mr Craddock,' Miss Malkin said as she came in, 'I wonder if I might . . .' she broke off what she was about to say and turned her pale eyes towards Davey. 'What a remarkably fine hand,' she said, smiling at him. 'Did you do that all by yourself? Or did you have some help . . .'

Her bright lipsticked smile widened as if at some secret joke shared just between them. Davey felt himself go weak. He went hot and cold at the same time while his heart hammered in his chest. He remembered the message on the slate. The rest of the class seemed to fade as Miss Malkin's eyes stared into him. *She* was the reason for Elizabeth's swift exit. Her eyes were the colour of pale winter dawns, bringing brightness but no warmth. Davey felt the blood drain from his face and his skin sheen with sweat. He felt faintly sick and had to cling to the desk.

'Davey Williams, isn't it?' Davey nodded feebly, his

head seemed barely connected to his neck. 'Well, well, I didn't realise you were so talented.'

She shook her head and her shiny dark hair flashed silver in the light. When he had seen her before, her hair had been the colour of frost. Now it was almost black and cut into a chin-length bob, maybe that was why he had failed to recognise her . . .

'I'm sorry, Mr Craddock.' She turned away, releasing the boy from her gaze to smile at the teacher now. 'I don't want to rush you, but my class is waiting . . .'

'Yes, of course. How thoughtless of me, I'm terribly sorry . . .' Craddock gushed. 'Right, you lot – out!' he yelled at the class before turning back to simper. Like most of the other male members of staff, he couldn't do enough for her.

They filed out past her class, which was lined up meekly outside. She didn't even look at Davey. He kept his head down, careful not to catch her glance. Her hair, her clothes, the way she talked, everything about her was right up to date. She even drove a car, he'd seen her in it. None of that mattered. Those were the eyes of the Lady, the Old Grey Man's daughter. Davey would know them anywhere. There could be no mistake.

# 3

Davey did not sleep well. He lay staring up at the ceiling; his head crowded with questions. What was the Lady doing here disguised as Miss Malkin? Was he right? Was it really her? Could he be mistaken? His mind careered in wild speculation; his thoughts seesawing between doubt and certainty. If it was her, what would she do to him? His insides seemed to congeal with fear at the thought of what she might have in store.

He got up to get a drink, wishing Kate was here. He could have talked to her. She had been there at midsummer and Hallowe'en, she knew the Lady and her powers. But Kate was at a sleepover, so no help there.

Davey left the door open, allowing light to come in from the landing. He tried again to settle down, to relax, but when sleep finally came it was anything but peaceful. Terrifying ghost crews chased him through dream after dream. The ones from Hallowe'en. A dirty white-robed figure leapt out at him, skeletal hands grabbed for him and the clown's mouth laughed, dripping redness, as Davey fled down an endless dark winding staircase, down to the dank cold cellar of Derry House. To the place where *she* was waiting, smiling, her long arms stretching out to him, waiting to . . .

He woke struggling, swallowing a sound somewhere between a muffled groan and a shriek. He untangled the sweaty sheets that had wrapped themselves around him and stayed awake, scared to sleep again, as the digits on the clock clicked towards morning. He lay rigid, unmoving, as light through the curtains and from the landing filled his bedroom with grotesque shadows and shapes. He listened, the hairs stirring on his head at every little creak, every little sound, trying to tell the natural from the uncanny.

He must have drifted off eventually. When he woke, weak winter light was filling the room. He rose immediately, dressing quickly. He did not want to spend another night like that. He badly needed to find Elizabeth.

He was at the museum just after it opened, turning the polished brass handle set in the solid oak door.

'You're bright and early,' the guide said as he came in. It was Mrs Summers, the one from yesterday, the one with the glasses on a chain round her neck and grey hair permed as neat as a lawyer's wig. 'Weren't you here with the school? Did you forget something?'

'Not exactly.' Davey stopped, she was standing in his path. 'I just wanted another look.'

'What are you interested in? You'll find the military section upstairs.' She began to rattle off the different exhibits before Davey could say anything. 'Or there's *The Victorian Schoolroom*, but I expect you had enough of that yesterday. *Dirt and Disease? The Way We Lived Then?*

Or you could try *The Blitz Experience*. It has only just opened.'

'I think I'll start over there, if that's OK.' Davey smiled and made towards the ground-floor room by the foot of the stairs.

'Please yourself. I was only trying to help.'

Davey went into the room at the base of the stairs and wandered round glass cases full of costumes, getting further from the entrance. Elizabeth had said that she would meet him here, but he was alone. He could find no sign of the ghost girl. The only sound in the quiet room was the ticking of long case clocks.

Davey was beginning to get anxious, afraid that she wouldn't show, when he heard a voice whisper, 'Over here, Davey! Over here!'

The glass cabinets reflected each other, like a series of mirrors. At the far end, a late Victorian/early Edwardian grey-green silk dress with velvet trim seemed to detach itself from its stand and come walking towards him.

They met in a corner, tucked away from the main exhibition area, in front of a door marked *Private*.

'Davey, I'm so glad you came.' Elizabeth put her small cold hand on his. 'As I told you yesterday, I have a message, and I feared I might not be able to deliver it.'

'If it's about Miss Malkin, about who she is, I already know. Yesterday afternoon, when she came into the room? I could tell.'

'Did you not suspect before?'

'No.' Davey shook his head. 'Not at all. She's new. She only came a few weeks ago and I don't have much to do with her, to be honest. Although . . .'

Davey fell silent, remembering Miss Malkin's first morning. She had been late. Assembly had already started. When she'd arrived, a cold blast of wind had caught the door and a bunch of withered leaves had swirled in with her. Davey had put it down to the weather. It could not have been long after Hallowe'en . . .

'Although?'

'Nothing,' Davey shook his head again. 'Just a few things beginning to make sense. You said you had a message.'

'Yes, from the Blind Fiddler. He says to tell you she means you the most terrible harm. He does not know the exact form it will take but she is seeking to create a trap in time . . .'

Davey froze. 'What does that mean?'

'I am not sure . . .' Elizabeth's brow wrinkled. 'He did try to explain, but I found his words hard to follow. It is all to do with magic and such. But this I do know.' Her grip on Davey's hand tightened. 'It is most tremendously serious. Much, much worse than anything else that could happen. If she catches you in this trap, you will neither live nor die. You will simply cease to exist. The only good thing is . . .'

Davey looked at her from his gathering despondency. 'There's a good thing?'

21

Elizabeth nodded. 'By doing this, she puts herself at risk. Also she acts without the permission of her father, the Old Grey Man himself.'

'Hmm.' Davey was far from comforted. 'Looks like she's going ahead, though. Or else why would she bother with all this Miss Malkin business?'

'Well, yes.' Elizabeth's frown deepened, but then she brightened. 'There is another thing. The trap will only work in a certain place, at a certain time, on a certain day of the year. So,' she spread her hands, 'it can be avoided. All you have to do is make sure that you are not there.'

'*Now* you tell me.' Davey's gloom lifted slightly. 'You had me worried back then.' That didn't seem at all bad. He had been imagining much worse. 'Just tell me where and when, and I'll make sure I'm not there.'

'The centre of the city.'

'Whereabouts? Old Town or New Town?'

'He didn't say . . .'

'He probably means the Old Town,' Davey said, thinking out loud. 'I mean, that's where everything happened when we went on the Haunts Ghost Tour. That shouldn't be too difficult to avoid . . . When is it supposed to happen?'

'The 12th.'

'That's next Friday. It's my birthday.' Davey frowned, his mind racing. 'Why then?'

'Because it's the solstice. The shortest day.'

'No, no.' Davey shook his head vigorously. 'You're

wrong. The solstice is the 21st, I'm sure. We've just done about it at school.'

'Not according to the old calendar and that's the one she goes by. The turning points of the year have special significance for the Host. You saw what happened at midsummer.' She shuddered. 'I have a feeling that midwinter is an altogether darker festival.'

'You mean she might want to use me as a—' he searched his mind for the word the Blind Fiddler had used. 'A teind, a tithe, a sacrifice?'

'Who is to say?' Elizabeth shrugged unhappily. 'Even the Fiddler cannot read what is in the Lady's mind when she is in her darker aspect. She becomes even more fey and unpredictable. Some say she has the power of wyrd, of fate itself. The power to reach through time, seizing the threads that link the future and the present to the past, twisting them to her own ends.' She paused for a moment. 'Perhaps that is what the Blind Fiddler meant. Tell me Davey, that girl you were with yesterday . . .'

'Lisa, you mean?'

'Yes. Did you tell her about me?'

'No chance.' Davey laughed at the thought of it. 'I lied and said I was on my own.'

'Oh? Why is that?'

'She doesn't believe in ghosts and stuff like that. She'd take the mickey.'

'Yet she saw me?'

'Ye-es . . .'

'Not just outside, but in the classroom, too. Don't you think that strange?'

'Mmm,' Davey nodded, he had thought it odd, though it had kind of slipped his mind. 'But she always says—'

'Those who protest the most, are often the most sensitive.'

'I hadn't thought of that . . .' he stopped and looked at her closely. 'Do you know what?' he said, his brown eyes scanning her face. 'I'd never noticed it before, but you look a lot like her.'

'Are you all right in there?' the guide's voice came in from the hallway. Davey cursed silently. There was so much more he wanted to ask but already Elizabeth was beginning to fade.

'Elizabeth.' Davey put out his hand to stop her. 'Don't go yet. Where will you be?'

'I must go. Don't worry. I will be here if you need me.'

'Where?'

'In the museum. It is as near as I can get to you. I will try to be here . . .'

'Whereabouts will you be?'

'Around. But I really must go now.'


'Who were you talking to?'

'No one.' Davey jumped guiltily, although Elizabeth had disappeared.

'Hmm.' The guide looked down at him, disapproving. 'Come out here a minute.' She led him into the hall.

24

Davey was ready to deny everything when she asked, 'Can you smell anything?'

Davey sniffed. 'No.'

'Well, I can. I smelt it yesterday. Just a whiff at the foot of the stairs.' She wrinkled her nose. 'Cigarette smoke.'

'Well, it wasn't me!' Davey's voice rose indignantly.

'I never said it was. Cleaners most likely. I'll have to have a word with the caretaker. It could set off the smoke alarms. I've told him before. There it is again.' She sniffed deeply. 'Are you sure you don't smell it?' Davey shook his head. There was a burst of male laughter from the military section. 'That does it.' She mounted the stairs. 'I'm going to find out what's going on up there.'

Davey watched her march up the polished stairs. Elizabeth's silvery laughter joined in the male guffaws. She must have gone back to the soldiers. The guide would never discover what was going on, never in a million years. Even if she did, people would say she had flipped. No one would ever believe her.

# 4

Just like they won't believe me either, Davey thought as he got outside and walked through the little garden and into the park.

He found a bench. He had to sit down. He felt oppressed. The day was grey and freezing and he felt as if something heavy and cold was lodged inside him, weighing him down. He really needed to talk to someone, plan how to avoid this thing that was going to happen, but it would have to be someone who already knew about the ghost city and the Lady. That meant Kate, or Tom, or Elinor. Kate was staying at her friend's house for the whole weekend and Tom and El lived too far away. It was not the kind of thing you could talk about on the phone.

Still, there was no need to panic, he told himself. Everything would be fine. All I've got to do is avoid the city centre on that particular night.

'Hi, Davey.' A voice cut into his thoughts, making him jump. 'What are you doing here?'

It was Lisa. She was swinging a sports bag and coming from the direction of school.

'Nothing.' Davey looked up at her through his dark fringe. 'I just came out for a walk. Where have you been?'

'At school. We've been rehearsing the Mummers' play.

I'm the Doctor. I cure St. George. Except he wasn't there. Billy Hawking is supposed to do it, but he fell off his bike last night—'

'Is he all right?'

'Yes, but he's chipped a bone in his elbow. He can't really come on with his arm in a sling. He has to fight the Turkish Knight, you see. The thing is, Davey . . .'

Lisa paused, scanning Davey's pleasant blunt-featured face, trying to gauge his reaction to what she was about to say. He was normally very easy-going, but he was no-body's pushover and he didn't like being taken for granted. He could be very stubborn if he wanted to be, and lately he had been acting rather strangely.

'The thing is what?' Davey asked, smiling at her hesitation.

'Well, the thing is,' she went on. 'The thing is, we need someone else—'

'So?' Davey shook his head, puzzled, he still had no idea what she was talking about.

'Well, the thing is . . .'

'You've said that four times already.'

'The thing is . . .'

'Five.'

'I suggested you.'

'What?' Davey stared at her, astonished.

'Well, you're really good at drama, and,' Lisa rushed on, before he could say anything, 'when they asked for suggestions, your name just popped into my head.'

'When's it for?' Davey knew about this vaguely, but hadn't taken much notice because he was not involved.

'Next week. We're going to act it out at the Victorian Evening because it's a traditional Christmas thing. There's to be a kind of pageant. Lots of schools are involved.'

'That's not much time—'

'I'll help you. It's simple. You don't have to do much at all. They've already got the costume and everything. There aren't many words to learn, it's mostly just miming.'

'Hey, wait—'

'Come on, Davey. Please say you will. We can't do it without St George. It's a major, major part and you'd be really good in it. Have a think about it. You don't have to decide till Monday . . .'

As Lisa talked on, Davey gradually warmed to the idea. He liked acting. He had been absent when they did the casting, otherwise he would probably have volunteered.

'I suppose I could think about it,' he said eventually. 'What exactly does it involve?'

High above them, at the top of the tall house which was now home to the museum, a small white face looked out from an attic window. Elizabeth watched the two friends talking. The girl, Lisa, interested her. She could feel a link, some kind of connection. Elizabeth's intuition told her that it could be significant, but how and why?

Elizabeth could not answer. Those things were still to be discovered, but they could be important. Intuition, not reason, ruled in the ghost world. She smiled slightly. The Old Grey Man's daughter was clever, but not that clever. They might still be able to outwit her. Her very arrogance left her open to attack from places she least expected.

To defeat her, Elizabeth had to find out more about what the Lady intended, and she could not do that by staying in the museum playing cards with the soldiers. She would have to find the Blind Fiddler, among others, and discover exactly what he knew. There was much to do. Despite her promise to him, it looked as if Davey would have to fend for himself. She stared down at the human boy she counted as a friend. He looked so small and isolated in the park's bleak winter landscape, so vulnerable. Perhaps she should stay, just in case he needed her. No. Her mind was made up. She would be more useful elsewhere. After all, she had given him fair warning, all he had to do was avoid the city centre.

'Come on, let's go.' Lisa gave a little shiver. 'It's getting cold.'

She shivered again, looking around her. It wasn't just the cold, she had an uncomfortable feeling, almost as if they were being watched.

'OK, I'm ready.' Davey stood up. 'Do you want to come back to my house – play on the computer?'

'I can't.' Lisa shook her head. 'I'm going Christmas shopping with my mum.'

'When is this play exactly?' Davey asked as they walked along.

'Victorian Evening, like I said.'

'What day is it?'

'Next Friday.'

'The 12th?'

'Yes. How do you know?'

'It's my birthday,' Davey said absently. Then he stopped walking. They were at the park entrance. There was a poster fixed to the tall, wrought-iron gates. It was as though it had been put there especially for him to see.

**Come to the Victorian Evening**
**12th December**
**City Centre**
**Late-Night Shopping**
**Various Stalls & Attractions**
**Carol Singing & Christmas Pageant**

'I can't do it,' he said as he read the notice. 'The play, I mean.'

'Why not?'

'Because – because it's my birthday,' he added quickly. 'My cousins are coming. I'll be doing something with my folks.'

'Oh, right.' Lisa shrugged. 'I'll just have to tell her.'

'Tell who?' Davey asked, although he already knew the answer.

'Miss Malkin. She's in charge of it,' Lisa replied. 'Didn't I say?'

# 5

Davey spent the rest of the weekend thinking that he had cracked it. He would get out of the Mummers' play by saying that he had to be somewhere that night, then all he had to do was avoid the city centre. He could divert Mum and Dad away from the Victorian Evening, even though they usually went to it, by saying he wanted to go somewhere different for his birthday, somewhere out in the country. Somewhere as far from the city as possible.

On Monday morning, Mr Craddock called him back after registration, but Davey was ready for him. He pretended to think for a while about being offered the part of St George, and then said,

'I'm afraid I can't do it, Sir.' His voice was tinged with exactly the right tone of regret.

'Oh? Why's that?' Craddock was taken aback, he had clearly not anticipated a refusal. 'Do you hear that, Miss Malkin?' he said over Davey's head. She had come up without him noticing. 'Davey here says he can't be in the Mummers' play.'

'Well, that is a shame . . .' the teacher's voice purred down towards him. 'And why might that be?'

'I – it's my birthday. M – my folks have something

special planned for me,' Davey stammered, staring down at the floor. He did not want to look at her and having her this close made him nervous.

'I thought that was the 13th?' Mr Craddock chipped in. 'That's what it says here,' he added, glancing down at the register.

'I – I was born at midnight,' Davey mumbled. 'They couldn't quite decide . . .'

'A chime child.' Miss Malkin smiled. 'That explains a lot of things,' she added under her breath, so only Davey heard it.

'Chime child? What's that then?' Mr Craddock asked, prepared to be impressed again. Her knowledge of folk-lore really was astonishing. He wondered if she had done a PhD, or something.

'Traditionally, a child born on a Friday as the clock chimes midnight has the ability to see ghosts, spirits and fairies – among other things . . .'

'Well, well, I didn't know that. Did you, Davey?' The teacher grinned down at Davey, who shook his head. 'Seen any lately?' The teacher guffawed at his own joke and Davey managed a weak smile. 'What a fund of knowledge you are Miss Malkin.' Mr Craddock turned back to his colleague. 'Particularly about all this stuff. The Head laps it up. He's a bit of a Morris man himself, been known to wave the odd handkerchief about.' He looked down at the boy. 'If you can't do it, can't be helped, I suppose. Run along. Now, you must tell me more,' he turned back to Miss Malkin. 'This kind of thing is *so* fascinating . . .

Davey did as he was told and trotted away, leaving Craddock to chat her up on their way to the staff room.

The feeling that he just might have got away with it lasted until afternoon registration. He was just filing in when Craddock caught hold of him.

'Excellent news, Davey.' The teacher's normally stern face was split in a genuinely happy smile. 'I had to pop up to the High Street this lunchtime, to do a bit of shopping.' Davey nodded, face fixed in a grin, wondering what the teacher's lunchtime activities had to do with him. 'And guess who I met?'

Davey shook his head, he couldn't possibly.

'Your mum!'

Davey nodded again, his grin still in place but his heart sinking fast.

'And – guess what?'

Davey shook his head weakly this time. His smile beginning to crumple at the thought of what was coming.

'I mentioned the Mummers' play,' Mr Craddock went on, oblivious to the different feelings flitting across Davey's face. 'And she said she'd be *very* happy for you to play St George. It won't interfere in your family plans at all. You were all going to the Victorian Evening anyway. She thought you knew that.'

'I must have forgotten,' Davey muttered.

'What?' the teacher cupped a hand round his ear.

'I must have forgotten,' Davey repeated, louder this time.

'So I can tell Miss Malkin all systems go.'

'Hmm,' Davey said, it was all he could manage.

'She'll be very pleased.' Craddock ignored him and beamed. 'She was most disappointed this morning, most displeased. She wanted you especially.' He put his arm round Davey's shoulder. 'And we wouldn't want to upset her, would we?'

'No,' Davey mumbled, staring at the lino tiles.

'Good lad.' the teacher grinned down at him, patting him on the back. 'I knew you wouldn't let me down. Now, there's a rehearsal after school—'

'But—'

'It's OK, it's OK,' he laughed, holding up his hands to damp down Davey's protest. 'I've cleared it with your mum, so there's no need to look so worried.'

'That's not what I'm worried about,' Davey muttered to himself.

'Say what?' The teacher cupped his ear again.

'Oh, nothing . . .'

'Righto, then.' Mr Craddock rubbed his hands together. 'That's sorted.'

Davey debated whether he should go home at three-thirty on the dot, pretending that he had forgotten, but that turned out not to be an option. Lisa sat by him all afternoon, so there was no chance of getting out of it like that.

He went with her to the hall as soon as the bell rang for the end of the day. Everyone involved in the pageant was there. Davey was surprised by the people he found. It wasn't just the ones who put their hands up for everything. Barry Jones was there with half the football team. They never usually volunteered for anything like this, but they seemed quite happy now, dressing up in strange costumes, waving handkerchiefs, dancing about and generally making total prats of themselves.

When he turned up with Lisa, Miss Malkin welcomed him with a smile, just like a normal teacher. She took him round, introducing him to the others, explaining what was going on. Not a flicker on her face gave her away, but all the time her eyes seemed to say: 'How are you going to get out of this one?'

There was none of the chaos which usually surrounded rehearsals for school performances. Everyone did exactly what they were told. No one messed about or answered back, not even Barry, who was well known for it. Miss Malkin did not have to shout, she did not even have to clap her hands to get quiet. One look did the trick. Davey watched as they all scurried to their places and waited quietly to be told what to do. They all hung on to her every word, grinning and simpering, wanting to please. They might as well have been a troupe of performing chimpanzees. Davey had never seen anything like this. It was truly scary.

Lisa had been right. He didn't have to do much at all. They all came in together and recited a verse, then each person stepped forward to say his or her bit. Davey was St George, so after his few lines he had to fight with Barry (who was the Turkish Knight), get killed, fall down and then get up again having been cured by Lisa.

They would all have special costumes to wear. Lisa wore a black frock coat and top hat, but the others wore coats sewn with bunches of cloth and ribbons and tall hats with fringes hanging from the brim. The purpose was to act as a disguise rather than to represent the player's role, Miss Malkin explained. The costumes were not quite ready yet. A group from her form was still working on them.

As Miss Malkin explained all this in her low musical voice, her magic began to work on him, too. Davey found himself wondering if he could be wrong. Maybe he was suffering from some kind of delusion. Here in the school hall, with its stacked chairs and scuffed floor and faint dinner smell, all the stuff Elizabeth had told him, even Elizabeth herself, seemed frankly unbelievable. Miss Malkin was pretty, attractive, charming and fun. That was the way all the other kids saw her; that was why they liked her. This might be unusual, but it did not make her anything other than an ordinary teacher.

They went through the action, rehearsing again and again. Davey quickly got the hang of it; he was even beginning to enjoy himself. It was a laugh. The time flew by. He couldn't believe it when the hall clock said half past five.

'Just one last thing, and we'll call it a day,' Miss Malkin said, clapping her hands to call them together. 'The Sword Dance. Barry, Sean.' Davey stood back as she called out the names of those involved. 'And you.' She took him by the shoulder and propelled him towards the centre of the forming group. 'We need you to be the Fool.'

'What do I have to do?' he asked.

'Nothing,' she smiled. 'Just stand in the middle. But stand quite still.'

Six boys came round him. The 'swords' they held in their hands were short lengths of steel, like metal rules. They began to pace in a clockwise direction, each boy crossing the hilt of his sword loosely over the point of his neighbour's. Davey stood still, as he had been told, watching the boys circle. None of them looked at him; they either looked at their sword or at the boy in front. When all the blades were crossed, the boys moved in so that the swords locked around Davey's neck.

'Why can't we use real swords, Miss? Instead of these things?' Barry asked as the lock began to tighten into a perfect hexagon.

'Because,' Miss Malkin laughed softly, and her pale eyes gleamed, 'if we did, we would cut Davey's throat. He would die in earnest. We wouldn't want that to happen, would we?' For some reason they all laughed. 'The Fool's death is purely a symbolic sacrifice. He just

falls to the floor when the dancers br⟨ ⟩
swords. Now!'

Davey stood, eyes wide, suddenly paralys⟨ ⟩
Steel rasped on steel, sharp and harsh in his ears,⟨ ⟩
boy pulled his sword away in a single swift withdr⟨ ⟩

'Very good. Excellently done.' She clapped her hands
again, in delight this time, and turned to Davey with a
smile. 'This is when you die, Davey.'

## 6

'I'm not going to do it, Lise,' he said as he walked her home.

'Why not? It's a good laugh. Especially the last bit, with the swords, you should have seen your face!' Lisa grinned at the memory.

'That's why I'm not going to do it.'

'What? Can't you take a joke?' Lisa looked at him. 'That's not like you, Davey.'

'It's not a joke, can't you see? That Miss Malkin – she's not who she says she is. She's out to get me.'

Lisa stopped walking. 'Not who she says she is?' Lisa repeated. 'Who on earth is she then? What *are* you talking about?'

'It would take too long to explain.' Davey shook his head and made to move on.

'Wait.' Lisa held his arm. 'You can't say a thing like that and just leave it.'

'Well, the thing is . . .' Davey paused, wondering how to start, weighing up whether to tell her or not.

He could wait and tell Kate, but she could be over at her friend's and not back until late. He needed someone to talk to now and Lisa was the best friend he had. Even though she was sceptical and said she did not believe in ghosts and things like that, he doubted she would accuse him of making it all up. She might even agree to help him get out of the mess he was in. After all, she had got him into it in the first place.

He told her all of it. About the Haunts Ghost Tour last summer and Jack Cade and his ghost crew, and the Old Grey Man's daughter.

'She came after me at Hallowe'en,' he went on. 'Because she wanted revenge . . .'

He told Lisa what had happened then and went on to explain his present fears. She was coming for him again, in the guise of Miss Malkin, and this time she was bound to get him. It all came out in a big long rush, but he might as well have saved his breath. He could tell by Lisa's face that she did not believe a word of it. By the end she wasn't even listening.

'You don't believe me, do you?' he said when he had finished.

'No.'

'But, Lise. I'm not making it up. Honest. I—'

'I don't want to hear any more. Ever. Save it, Davey.' She was walking away from him. 'Either you *are* making it up, or you're crazy. Everybody knows there are no such things as ghosts – let alone *fairies*!'

'But it isn't just me!' Davey protested. 'What about Kate? And Tom and Elinor—'

'They must be crazy, too. You must all be suffering from the same delusion.'

41

'But, Lisa—'

'I'm not listening, Davey.' She put her hands over her ears, shaking her head. 'Ghosts aren't like that,' she said quietly, almost to herself. 'They aren't highwaymen and fairy queens.'

'Oh?' Davey was watching her closely now. 'What are they, then?'

'I'm not telling you!' Lisa almost shouted back. 'Like I said, there are no such things! You are all big liars!'

She ran off down the road, leaving him to walk home alone. Davey watched her go. He did not try to stop her. The strength of her feeling had shaken him. He would get no help from her, that was obvious; but, still, her reaction was curious. Despite what she said, Davey had a feeling that Lisa had particular reasons for not believing, reasons that she was not prepared to share with him or anyone else.

The next day, Mum gave him a lift to school. She talked nonstop about how wonderful it was that he would be in the Mummer's play, and how she and Dad were *really* looking forward to it. Davey did not reply. He got out of the car with the feeling that things were closing in around him; as though nothing would get him out of this pageant.

He tried all day, but Miss Malkin had covered every angle. It did not help that everybody else thought she was wonderful. The Head did a special assembly and sat and beamed while she talked about all these folky Christmas customs. At the end he said what a splendid job she was doing, and how important he considered the pageant to be for school prestige. He didn't need to add what a dim view he'd take if anyone tried to bail out of it.

It was just as bad with Davey's own class. Miss Malkin was equally popular with them. Davey was the only one to think there was anything strange about her. Craddock was following her around like a lovesick spaniel; doing everything short of rolling over and doing tricks. All the other kids thought she was the best thing since sliced bread. They wouldn't hear a word against her. To make matters worse, Lisa wasn't even talking to him. She was hanging around with people Davey didn't like, leaving him feeling left out and isolated.

On his way home Davey slipped into the museum, hoping to see Elizabeth, hoping that she could help him. He wandered around from one room to another but he could not find her.

He ended up in a small room off the first landing. All around the walls were black-and-white photographs and glass cases filled with gas masks, tin hats and ration books. The centre of the room was taken up by a large glass cabinet, housing the city in miniature relief with the river snaking through it.

There was no sign of Elizabeth here. He was just about to leave, when suddenly the lights went out. The whole room was filled with a mournful wailing sound.

A deep male voice boomed out: '*Welcome to Manor Museum's Blitz Experience.*'

Davey felt waves of panic sweeping over him; he had to resist a very strong temptation to throw himself to the floor.

'*We will take you back to the night of 12th December 1940, when wave after wave of enemy bombers brought devastation to the city.*'

Davey looked round in desperation. He thought for a moment that the voice was inside his own head.

'*The city moved to red alert as a full moon, a Raider's Moon, rose brilliant in the dark night sky, turning night into day, lighting the way for the enemy bombers . . .*'

The siren wailed even louder and lights began to probe the darkness inside the large glass cabinet. The rumble and engine whine of many planes crept under the blanketing moan. Backlit shadows appeared, German bombers, Heinkels and Junkers, projected on to the wall.

'*The first wave of planes dropped incendiaries. Fire bombs rained down marking the city out as a clear target for the bombers following . . .*'

Red light erupted all across the darkened cityscape; clusters of buildings glowing and fading in random patterns, until the whole central area was a rolling mass of fire.

'*Then came the high explosives . . .*'

More red lights, this time synchronised with thumps and crumps on the sound track.

'*Until the entire centre of the city was one massive conflagra-tion, with hardly a building standing. The burning city was visible as a glow in the sky forty miles away . . .*'

Davey stood in the centre of the room as the disem-bodied voice went on, itemising the destruction: the number of planes used, the tonnage of bombs dropped, the number dead and missing, the areas flattened beyond recognition, the buildings gone forever, or damaged beyond repair. He wanted to make a break for it, but he couldn't move, he had to stay and listen. He felt the familiar shivering skin-crawl feeling of premonition, but this was worse. He was pale, sweating, and trembling all over.

It was like that time when he had nearly been run over. Whenever he remembered, he lived through it again. The moment was frozen in his memory, complete with screeching of brakes, people shouting, the world dissol-ving to horrible slow motion as the car travelled towards him. It was like that, but worse. A premonition in reverse. He was caught up in some terrible episode from the past, which had yet to happen. As he watched, he felt as though he was trapped inside the glass box.

'Impressive, isn't it?'

Davey jumped at the sound of the guide's voice. It was Mrs Summers, the one he had seen before. She had been standing by the door watching him.

'Umm, yeah.' The words came out in a hoarse mur-mur.

'Some of our older visitors have a very powerful reaction, especially to the siren. Brings back the memories like nothing else. That raid was the first – and the worst.' She went on in the face of Davey's silence. 'We weren't expecting it, you see. London, Coventry, Bristol, then us. It was terrible, terrible.' She shuddered, pulling her knitted jacket closer. 'I was just a little kiddie – but I remember that night as if it were yesterday.'

She stopped speaking and stared into the model of the burning city, listening to the end of the commentary. As the lights played across her face, her mouth compressed and her cheeks creased, puckering into lines of sadness and sorrow.

The overhead light went on and the voice faded but still Davey could not escape. The woman took him round, showing him the photographs taken after the event. The King and Queen surrounded by heaps of rubble; buses and tram cars tossed on their sides, lying about like discarded toys; the long communal graves in what is now the Peace Garden. Davey had seen much of this before, he had done a project at school, but right now he didn't want to look any more. He felt strange. Sick to his stomach. As though he was going to faint.

'Thanks for showing me,' he muttered. 'But I have to go . . .'

'That's all right.'

The guide eyed him curiously as he left the gallery.

That boy showed all the signs of having been through the blitz himself. He was pale, sweating. When the siren had started he had jerked like a puppet, but how could he remember? His mother had probably not even been born . . .

'Pretend you're ill.'

This was Kate's advice when he explained the situation to her. She was thirteen, going on fourteen, and went to the upper part of the school so she had not met Miss Malkin, but she had met the Old Grey Man's daughter and knew her talent for disguise. Kate had seen the things Davey had seen. She had been with him in the ghost city at midsummer, and at Hallowe'en. She had been through it before.

'Have you told anyone else?' she asked after giving Davey's problem a little more thought.

'Only Lisa. I – I thought that I ought to – she got me into it after all.'

'What did she say?'

'Said I was crazy.'

'Wait a minute.' Kate turned on her brother. 'You didn't tell her about the rest of it. What happened to us, I mean. At midsummer and Hallowe'en . . .'

'Might have. A bit,' Davey said miserably.

'Oh, Davey.' Kate rolled her eyes to the ceiling. 'I thought we agreed, the day after Hallowe'en – you, me, Tom and Ellie – we'd never tell anybody.' They found it hard enough to believe it themselves, never mind trying to convince anybody else. 'How did she take it?'

'Er, not well,' he said unhappily. 'I think I touched a raw nerve . . .'

Davey tailed off. He regretted their conversation now. He hadn't wanted to lose a friend over it, but thought he might have done just that.

'Well, like I said.' Kate sighed. 'You'll just have to pretend you're ill, and hope Lisa doesn't say anything.'

'What? Like start now? Tell Mum I've got a sore throat coming on?'

'No,' Kate shook her head. 'That'd be too soon. Thursday. Then you won't have time to get better. Come home tomorrow saying you've not been well at school, then you can be away the next day. It has to be bad, but not too bad. Not a sore throat or a rash,' she added. 'Nothing Mum can look at. Something like,' Kate thought for a bit, 'headache, stomach pains, feeling sick, general achiness. Maybe not the whole lot or Mum'll panic and call in the doctor.'

Davey took Kate's advice. That night he became quiet and subdued and went to bed early complaining of a headache. He put on an act all the next day at school, which wasn't very difficult. They had a rehearsal at dinner time. He only had to think about the swords tightening round his neck to feel sick. By Wednesday evening, his mum didn't take much convincing that he was going down with something.

'You'd better stay home tomorrow, then,' she said, putting her hand on his forehead. 'That way we can make absolutely sure that you'll be all right for Friday and the Mummers' play.'

## 7

Everything was going fine until Thursday night. Davey was feeling safe. He had rather enjoyed his day in bed. Then the phone went. Davey padded downstairs to answer the call. It was Lisa.

'Are you coming in tomorrow?'

'I don't know. I might not feel like it.'

'Please, Davey. Miss Malkin will cancel the play if you don't show.'

'Can't she get somebody else?'

'No. Too short notice. She'll withdraw us from the pageant—'

Davey did not reply. Normally he would do anything to help Lisa out, but this time he could not oblige. The risk was just too great.

'There's nothing wrong with you, is there?' Lisa asked into the silence.

'Yes, of course there is. I'm – I've got,' Davey floundered, even over the phone he found lying to her difficult.

'Got what? Bunkoffitis?' Lisa's voice was cold with angry contempt. 'You're a coward and you're going to let everybody down. The school, your friends – some of us have worked hard for this. Not just rehearsing, but making all the costumes and props.'

'I know, Lisa,' Davey groaned, 'but—'

'But nothing,' Lisa's voice hissed down the phone. 'You just can't do this, Davey.'

Davey thought for a while, his mind searching frantically for another excuse, another reason why he could not go.

'I can't be there, anyway,' he said finally, trying a different tack, just to get her off his back. 'Tom and El are coming over and we're all going to that new place outside Kingswood,' he lied. 'It's really brilliant, not like the boring Victorian Evening. You can play on all sorts of stuff and eat as much as you want. It's going to be my birthday treat.'

It was the worse thing he could have said.

'Oh, really?' Lisa's voice was wobbly with unshed tears. 'Well, have a nice time, Davey.'

'I will, don't worry,' Davey replied to an empty line.


Lisa put down the phone before tears betrayed her further. Her hand trembled as she replaced the receiver. She had never felt this angry before with anyone, let alone Davey. Normally they were the best of friends, but now all her feelings for him were curdling inside her, transforming from anger to chilling contempt at his cowardly self-ishness. If he thought he was going to some entertainment centre tomorrow night, he had another think coming. If he wasn't at school, first thing, she was going to Miss Malkin. Her grey eyes gleamed at the thought of telling the teacher what Davey was *really* up to . . .

Let's see him get out of that, then, Lisa thought to herself, her resolve strengthening as the evening went on. She had never grassed on anyone before; but this was different; for this she was prepared to break the unwritten code of classroom and playground. Her lips curled in a private smile of triumph at all the trouble heading his way.

It never crossed her mind that her anger was anything other than justified. She did not think, as she prepared for bed, that there might be some other force at work, worming a way between her and Davey, poisoning their friendship. It did not occur to her that the thoughts corrupting her mind, corroding her feelings for her friend, replacing affection with loathing and contempt, belonged to anyone but herself.

'Lisa! Lisa!'

Lisa lay quite still, trying not to listen to the voice talking to her from the end of the bed. The voice was light and small, whispery and thin, like the rubbing of insect wings.

'Lisa. Lisa. You must listen to me.'

Lisa lay rigid. The voice belonged to nothing human. It rustled like dry husks, it whistled in and out of range like a shortwave radio set. This must be a dream, she told herself. I am dreaming. I am dreaming. I am dreaming. She repeated the words over and over again in her head and kept her eyes tight shut. Keeping her eyes shut was important. To open them, would make this reality. She would have to believe what she had denied for so long. Because this had happened before. Once when she was very small.

She had heard her name called, just like this, although the voice was stronger then, more recognisably human. She woke to find him standing by her bed, looking down at her. An old man, looking just like he did in life, wearing dark trousers and a white shirt, and the old brown cardigan he wore to do the garden. She had not been frightened. Not then.

'Hello, Grandpa,' she had said. 'What are you doing here?'

He smiled, but all he'd said was, 'Goodbye.'

In the morning she'd gone downstairs looking for him, asking where he was. Her mum, already pink-eyed, ran from the kitchen sobbing. It was left up to her dad to explain that Grandpa was dead. They had just received a phone call. He had passed away at four o'clock that morning.

The shock was hard to describe. It was the first time in Lisa's life that anyone had died. She never told anybody about what happened that night. The years blurred the truth, allowing her to believe it was a dream, that she had imagined it. Now it was happening again. Lisa shut her mind along with her ears and eyes until the alarm clock heralded the morning.

# 8

Davey stayed in bed, still suffering from vague flu-like symptoms. It was his birthday, but that was all right, about lunchtime he planned on making a miraculous recovery. He snuggled down under the duvet, listening to the rest of the family preparing to leave for work and school. Dad had already left. Mum was shouting for Kate and Emma to get ready.

'It's almost half past.' She sounded distinctly irate. 'Hurry up or you'll both be late.'

'Coming, Mum,' Emma's voice came from the landing. He heard his younger sister's feet patter down the stairs.

Just as she reached the bottom, the phone rang.

'Hello?' She listened for a second. 'Hang on. I'll just get her. Mum!' Emma's voice floated down the hall to the kitchen. 'It's for you!'

'Hello? Yes, speaking . . .'

Mum's voice now. Davey sat up, his skin crawling with unnamed dread.

'Kate! Kate!' He got out of bed and padded to his sister's room.

Kate was at her dressing table, applying discreet traces of make-up.

'Happy birthday, Davey,' she said, without looking round.

'Never mind that now.' His birthday was the last thing on his mind.

'Please yourself.' Kate returned to her mascara.

'Who's that on the phone?'

'How do I know?'

Davey shivered. 'I've got a feeling. I think it might be Malkin.'

Kate's face changed from annoyance to concern.

'Hold on. Emma might know. Emma?'

Emma came out of her room.

'Happy birthday, Davey,' she said looking up at her brother.

'Thanks,' he said absently. 'Who's that on the phone to Mum?'

'I don't know . . . I'm not sure . . .' Emma thought for a second, then added, 'I think it might be Miss Malkin. I recognised her voice from assembly. She doesn't shout like the others . . .'

'I told you!'

Davey and Kate crouched at the top of the stairs, peering through the banisters, keeping out of Mum's line of vision, but in a position where they could hear her conversation. Mum was not saying much. Her responses were limited to, 'Unhn' 'I see', 'yes, of course', 'I understand', but her tone of voice was changing from puzzlement, to concern, and finally anger. Kate and Davey pulled back as every now and then she shot a look upstairs to the bedrooms.

'Of course,' she said finally. 'I quite understand. No, no, thank *you* very much for informing me. Oh, no trouble, Miss Malkin. No trouble at all.'

Kate and Davey scattered to their different rooms as she put down the receiver. She stood for a moment, her jaw tightening. Then she turned for the stairs.

'Davey! You get out of bed right this minute! You're going to school. Kate! Emma! What are you still doing here? You should be out by now. How many times do you have to be told?'

'Can we have a lift, Mum?' Emma asked brightly, failing to understand what was going on.

'No, you can't.'

'O-oh. What about Davey? He's not ready.'

'Don't worry about your brother.' Alison Williams stared at his closed bedroom door, her face grim. 'He's going in under personal escort.'

When they got to school, Davey's mum came in and took him to the secretary's office.

'I'm sorry he's late,' she said with a tight smile. 'But he is feeling better, *much* better. Aren't you, Davey?'

Davey looked down at the ground, scuffing his feet, pretending not to see the look that passed between the two adults. In the hall behind him, the dress rehearsal had started. Just when he was thinking things could not get any worse, they did.

'Mrs Williams, isn't it?' he heard a voice say. 'How do you do? I'm Miss Malkin. We spoke on the phone. I'm so glad that Davey's recovered enough to join us.' She put her hand on his shoulder. 'We were rather worried.' She smiled her immaculate lipstick smile. 'We *are* so relying on him. He does have rather an important part!'

The two adults laughed together, although Davey failed to see anything remotely funny in Miss Malkin's last remark.

'Don't you worry, Miss Malkin.' Davey's mum looked at the teacher, her voice grimly serious again. 'He'll be there tonight. You can count on it. I give you my word.'

Behind him he could hear the sword lengths slide and lock together. It felt as if they were tightening round his heart.

# 9

'Nothing will happen. We won't let it, will we?' Kate appealed in a whisper to Tom and Elinor, their twin cousins who had come over to help celebrate Davey's birthday. They had all come into the city centre together. Kate casually edged away from where Mum and Dad were standing with Emma to make it easier to talk.

'Not a chance,' Tom grinned down at his cousin. Although only a year older, he was nearly a head taller. 'We're with you now, mate.'

'Have you heard anything more from Elizabeth?' Elinor asked.

Davey shook his head. Having them there was a big help, but he was still very worried.

'There you are, then,' Elinor went on, smiling her reassurance. 'If it was really *that* dangerous she'd have been back in contact.'

'Yes, I suppose . . .'

'It'll be all right, Davey.' Elinor took his hand. 'Nothing's going to happen.'

'No, because like Kate says, we won't let it.' Tom flicked his sandy fringe out of his eyes, scanning the crowds. 'First sign of trouble from her, or anything unusual happening, and we'll be over to sort it out.'

They were standing on Bridge Street, looking down into the gardens by the river. All around them the town centre was filling up. The Victorian Evening was a popular pre-Christmas retailing event, loyally supported by shop-keepers and public alike. Many of the people crowding the streets were dressed in period costume, carrying little lanterns. All the shops were open, many of them offering hot mince pies, punch and mulled wine, free to the public. Usually Davey enjoyed the atmosphere. He liked to see the familiar streets transformed to an approximation of a hundred years ago, set out with stalls and sideshows, but this year the only thing he could think about was the possibility of escape. Despite having Kate and Tom and Elinor with him, he almost thought of running away, disappearing into the crowd, coming back later when the danger was over, but something told him that even that would be futile. Somehow he was trapped. He felt like a rat in a maze. All roads would lead back here.

Down below him, companies of performers were already beginning to assemble. The River Gardens formed a natural amphitheatre. Crowds were gathering, looking over the railings from Broad Street and down from the New Bridge which led to Can-nongate on the other side of the dark river. Over there, the Old Town rose up. The floodlit cathedral and the steep roofs forming a natural backdrop to the action to be played out below.

Davey could see his school troupe. Lisa was there with her doctor's bag and top hat. Mr Craddock was fussing round dressed in his Jekyll and Hyde coat, ticking off the boys having mock fights with the rappers, the short lengths of steel they used in the sword dance. Davey squinted down at the excited children milling around, his forehead creased in an anxious frown. He could not see Miss Malkin anywhere among them.

'It'll be all right.' His mum smiled down at him and squeezed his shoulder. She had stopped being angry with him and had put his reluctance down to stage fright. 'I'm sure they are all as nervous as you are. Perhaps you'd feel better if you went down and joined them.'

'I don't want to go yet,' Davey mumbled. 'We won't be on for ages.'

He felt like a condemned man. He glanced round gloomily for Kate, Tom and Elinor, but even they seemed to have deserted him. They had gone off on their own somewhere. Despite what they'd said about sticking by him, they had left him here with Mum and Dad. He was not impressed by that. They could have at least stayed to keep him company. He stared down moodily, picking at the paint on the railing with his thumb nail.

'Davey! Hey, Davey! Over here!'

He looked up sharply at his name being called. At first he thought it was coming from down in the garden, that they were calling him at last, but no one there was looking in his direction. He searched across the railings, scanning the people gathering on the bridge and his heart leapt. Kate was there, with Tom and Elinor. They were beckoning him over. Kate's face was transformed with excitement, her eyes were shining, she was grinning from ear to ear. At first Davey failed to see what all the fuss was about, then he saw the people with her. Not just any people, not even people in the strictest sense. Somehow she had managed to locate the ghost crew. *Their* ghost crew: Jack Cade the highwayman, with Polly by his side, Elizabeth was there, too, and the mute boy, Govan. They were standing like a family group; their strange clothes blending with all the others in fancy dress. And there at the back, standing with his hand on Govan's shoulder, was the Blind Fiddler.

Davey smiled, relief flooding through him in great waves. It was as if a huge weight had been lifted from him. Somehow Kate had found them all, even the Blind Fiddler. Just in the nick of time, they had come to save him. His troubles were over.

He was just about to go and join them when a voice behind him said, 'I don't know where you think *you're* going, young man,'

And a heavy hand came down on his shoulder.

## 10

'I think you're wanted down there.' Davey's father nodded towards the gardens below. 'Looks like it's showtime.'

Davey felt his doom come upon him. The other participants had stopped their aimless milling. Mr Craddock was frantically waving in his direction. Each school had been separated out and marshalled into different areas. The pageant was about to begin. Davey's group stood quiet and subdued, waiting their turn like everyone else. Right in the middle of them stood Miss Malkin, tall and slender, dressed in a long gown of some dark rich material. Her head was circled with a narrow band of gold, and she wore a white star on her brow. She was looking every inch the Fairy Queen, the King of Elfland's daughter.

'Mr and Mrs Williams! So nice to see you here.' Miss Malkin extended her hand to both of them. 'Thanks so much for coming, and for bringing Davey.' Her long slim fingers slipped to his shoulder. 'We wouldn't get very far without him.' Her shark-like smile widened. 'He's the star of our show!'

'It's a pleasure.' Alison Williams smiled back. 'We've been looking forward to it. I must say, I like your outfit.'

She stood back to admire the teacher. Miss Malkin's long flowing gown was of deep green velvet. The soft rich material clung to her figure. She wore a silver torc round her white throat and a gold chain in the form of a snake looped down from her slender waist. A golden chaplet circled her shining hair; a single stone glimmered white on her forehead.

'Every year I intend to dress up but I never get round to it,' Alison Williams went on. 'You look wonderful, like something out of a Pre-Raphaelite painting, doesn't she?' She nudged her husband. 'Doesn't she, Stephen?'

Stephen Williams just nodded. He was standing like a stunned calf, just staring at the teacher.

'Ah, Mr and Mrs Williams, so nice to see you—'

Mr Craddock was coming across now to join the Miss Malkin Admiration Society. Davey looked around warily. Kate and the others were still standing on the bridge looking over the railings. Maybe he could make a dash for it. If he could get away from her and back to them, then maybe they could save him. Davey tensed his body, ready for action, and felt the long fingers increase their grip on his shoulder, the nails digging in like knives.

'If you'll excuse us,' she addressed Davey's mother, her head tilted slightly back, heavy eyelids masking her slanting eyes. 'I just want a private word with Davey.'

'Of course . . .' his mother replied, held by her gaze. She hadn't noticed before, and didn't mean to stare, but this woman's eyes really were the most extraordinary colour. The shade seemed to shift and slide from rain-water-grey, to a pale green, as clear as a precious stone.

'Are you sure there's time?' Mr Craddock looked at his watch.

'Oh, there's enough time, don't worry,' Miss Malkin looked down at Davey. 'We won't be long. I just want to borrow him for a while.'

'You can have him with pleasure.' Davey's father laughed. 'How about for ever?'

The remark was meant as a joke, but it seemed to shiver in the air, echoing as if the short space between them was an immense gulf.

Davey wanted to scream, 'No, Dad! No!'

But he could find no voice. The words stayed lodged in his throat.

The Lady gave a deeper smile. Her pale tilted eyes ignited with white fire as she took Davey by the shoulder and led him towards the darkness at the edge of the crowd.

## 11

'You've got to do something!'

Kate was frantic. She turned to the ghost crew for help but they all stood, motionless, witnessing Davey's walk to the performance area. Tears sparkled in Polly's eyes and Jack's face was dark with rage. The Blind Fiddler's blank eyes turned up to the sky. Govan looked down at the dark water rushing beneath his feet and Elizabeth closed her eyes, as if she couldn't bear to see what was happening.

'Please!' Kate went from one to the other, pleading. 'You've got to help him!'

At last the Blind Fiddler spoke.

'There is nothing we can do. The Lady is in her dark aspect and she has worked her magic well. We are powerless this side of the water.' His head turned to the mass of the Old Town that lay on the other bank of the river. 'We shouldn't even be here.'

'What will she do to him?' Elinor asked quietly.

'She has woven a trap for him,' the Blind Fiddler explained. 'There are certain places, at certain times, where even ghosts cannot venture. To do so is to risk perpetual oblivion. Down there is one such.'

He nodded towards the sunken garden. The children stared, incredulous, it seemed so innocent. It was a such a peaceful place, especially in summer, with its long walks down by the river, flanked by benches and grass areas and wide flower beds.

'I know what you are thinking,' the Fiddler added, 'but it was not always so. This was not always an empty space. Once there were busy streets, home to many people. Small houses crowded right down to the river, jostling for space with shipping offices and warehouses.'

Kate went white. 'I think – I think I know.'

'What is it? What happened?' Tom and Elinor turned to her. They were not from the city and knew little of its history.

Kate said nothing, she just pointed over their heads. *Memorial Peace Garden* was spelt out in wrought iron letters, arched above the steps.

'Memorial to what?' Tom still didn't understand.

'There was a terrible air raid, in World War Two.'

'Like the one we saw in the summer?'

Kate nodded. 'Worse than that. We learned about it in History. It happened in December, as far as I remember . . .' She turned to the Fiddler. 'This is the anniversary, isn't it?'

The old man nodded.

'But – but –' Kate shook her head, unwilling to accept the implication. 'Tom's right. We witnessed the same thing last summer and we still got through—'

'We were on the other side of the bridge then. This would be different. If I read the Lady's intentions correctly, she plans to send Davey right into the heart of it. At such times, fire seals the city. We cannot enter. We would be consumed in an instant.'

'What about Davey?' Kate's lips were trembling. 'Is that – is that what will happen to him?'

The Fiddler's blind eyes rolled towards her and his creased and weathered face held a look of infinite sadness.

'I really do not know what fate she has in store for him.' His shoulders slumped and he bowed his head as though suddenly overcome with great weariness. 'I'm sorry, my dear.'

'We can't just do nothing,' Tom said impatiently. He'd had enough of this defeatist talk. 'I'm going down there now.' He made for the steps. 'I'm going to get him back.'

'Wait!' the Fiddler commanded. 'There is nothing you can do. Nothing. To accomplish her ends she has twisted the strands of fate itself. However you try to intervene, whatever you do, something will prevent you.' He turned to Kate. 'I should imagine Davey tried hard not to be here tonight?'

Kate nodded. 'Yes, he tried every way.'

'Just so. She has made it his fate, his *wyrd*. Something neither the Living nor the Dead can prevent.' He shook his head sadly. 'Nothing can stop what will happen. What will be, will be. All we can hope is that Davey might somehow survive.'

He put his hand to his mouth, his blind eyes rolling as his chin sank to his chest. Whatever his words, his expression did not seem to rate Davey's chances very highly. Govan patted his master's arm. The tremble of the hand on his shoulder told of the old man's distress.

The rest of the ghost crew felt helpless just standing by, but if the Blind Fiddler could not aid the boy, they were even more powerless. Polly turned her head into Jack's chest. She was fond of Davey and could not bear to think about the cruel fate that the Lady had devised for him.

Jack put his arm round her and stared down at the scene below, stony faced. He had helped Davey at Hallowe'en, but that had been fighting something he could see. The Lady herself. All this talk of fate and *wyrd*, Jack shivered. He hated the Old Grey Man's daughter because she was everything he most feared. Give him good honest ghosts any day. His hand tightened on his sword – he knew how to deal with them. These others, the Host, the Unseelie Court, with their slippery magic and their treacherous ways; at the thought of them his nostrils flared, he hated the very smell of *Faerie*.

'There is one way . . .'

The ghosts all turned to Elizabeth. She had not explained her idea to them. She was still far from sure that it would even work and the Blind Fiddler had counselled against it because of the risk to herself. But if someone didn't do something, and soon, it would be too late.

She leaned over the rails, gazing down at the scene below, tracking the main players. Davey was still with his parents. The Lady was there, smiling at them, her attention distracted. Elizabeth scanned the other children, looking for the girl, Lisa. There she was, standing slightly apart. Elizabeth's grip on the rail tightened and she tensed with sudden excitement.

She turned to Kate. 'D'you see that girl down there, the one with the bag and the top hat?'

'Lisa?'

'Yes. Go and get her.'

'What for? She doesn't even believe—'

'Even so. She's the only one who can help him now.'

'But how? I don't see—'

'Just do as I say.' Elizabeth shook her head, denying Kate's protests. 'We do not have time to argue, just go.'

'Oh, all right,'

'There *is* a connection,' Elizabeth addressed the Blind Fiddler as Kate made for the steps.

He inclined his head. 'I understand. But do *you* understand the risk you take?'

'Yes.'

'Very well.' The blind man nodded his blessing, but his face remained creased with anxiety. 'I only hope you are right.'

'I am, I know it. Bring her up here to me,' Elizabeth called down to Kate. 'And hurry!'

Hurry indeed, the Blind Fiddler thought, his face resuming its sombre lines as the girl's light feet tapped away down the metal steps. While you still remember that you have a brother . . .

69

'Lisa! Lisa! Come here!' Kate beckoned the girl away from her companions. 'You've got to come with me.'

'What?' Lisa turned, surprised to see Davey's sister waving at her and whispering fiercely. 'I can't. It's about to start any minute.'

'They'll have to start without you, then.' Kate was pulling her arm now, dragging her out of the crowd.

'Hang on, Kate. Just a minute! What do you think you're doing?'

'Someone wants to speak to you. It's about Davey.'

'What's the matter with him? Is he in some kind of trouble?'

'You could say that. And you're the only one who can help him out.'

'But why?' Lisa frowned. 'He seems all right now. I've just seen him over there with your mum and dad, talking to Miss Malkin and Craddock . . .'

Her voice tailed off. Davey was no longer where she thought he was. His parents were still with Mr Craddock, but Miss Malkin and Davey seemed to have slipped off. Lisa turned and looked around, searching the crowd, but the boy and his teacher were nowhere to be seen.

# 12

'Why have you brought me here?' Davey's voice was flat and toneless. He walked with her like an automaton. He no longer thought of shouting or running away. He felt numb all over. The heaviness round his heart was almost unbearable and his legs felt like lead.

They had moved away from the area that had been set up for performance, out into the dark quietness of the far side of the garden. Somewhere close, the river lapped and flowed. Coloured lights moved in the sliding black water, reflected from the Christmas lights strung above the soaring concrete bridge. Davey was reminded of the dazzling bridge he had seen in the summer. Then it had meant deliverance, an end to danger. Now the twinkling lights seemed to wink and mock at him, like will o' the wisp fairy lights, signalling the opposite.

'I have something to show you.'

The Lady was leading him away from the river now. They moved across grass crisping with frost and stopped in front of a small garden set out with ornamental trees and benches. As they left the glare of artificial street lights, Davey was aware of the prickle of stars above him, and the bright, cold glow of moonlight casting shadows. When they had left home, the night had been overcast, heavy with cloud.

'Is this what you want to show me?'

They had stopped in front of a monument. Moonlight shone on white marble surrounded by the gaunt black shapes of trees stripped of their leaves. They seemed to bend over, reaching down, weeping at what they were seeing. A little shelf, like a plinth, stood in front of the listed names. It held poppy wreaths, blood-red petals reduced to black by the strange, pale light. They lay next to little wooden crosses and withered bouquets, faded bunches of flowers rotting inside glinting cellophane.

'You know what this is?'

'Yes,' Davey said, 'it is a war memorial.'

'Who for? Do you know?'

'The civilian dead of the city, killed in air raids in the Second World War.' Davey knew that too, he had visited this very place as part of a school project his class had done last year. 'I've seen it before.'

'Have you? Did you read the names?'

'Yes.'

'Look again.' Her long finger pointed. 'Look down there.'

Davey leaned nearer. She was indicating a section towards the base of the monument. Moonlight glimmered on the white stone, making the carved letters hard to read:

Chapel Street Shelter, 12th December, 1940.

'What is underneath?'

'Names. A list of names.'

'And at the bottom?'

'*Mr Harry Hamilton*,' Davey read out, '*Air Raid Warden.*'

He glanced at the list above. There were Hamiltons named there, too. *Hamilton, Sarah G.* and *Hamilton, Sylvie, aged six months*.

'What else?'

Davey had to bend right over to read the letters at the base.

'*Five persons unidentified, including two children. May they forever rest in peace.*' He turned from the inscription to look up at her. 'I don't see . . .'

'Oh, you will, Davey. You will.'

She smiled down at him, her teeth shining bright in the moonlight. She had shed any vestige of Miss Malkin. On her pale brow, the white stone gleamed, lit from deep within by sparks of blue and green. The gold circlet glittered in her hair like fire on frost. Her cheek bones showed like blades as she turned her face to the sky. Cold flames leapt in her silver eyes. Exultation surged through her and she allowed herself a moment of pure pleasure. She had used High Magic to create this enchantment, to catch this wily chime child, to unpick the threads of fate and trap him in the web of time. Now she would be rid of him forever. The spell was wound up.

73

'Do not look for help,' her voice whispered down to him. 'You are beyond the aid of anyone, the dead or the living.'

'What do you mean?' Davey managed to speak, although the terror he felt was enough to paralyse him. It spread through him, until he could not even blink his eyes.

'You don't exist, Davey.' Her laughter shivered to the stars and beyond. 'Nothing can help you now.'

As he watched, her tall slender figure seemed to grow even higher. She threw her head back to the sky and let out a high, keening, wailing cry, calling in a language without words, pure sibilant sound. Her dress shimmered until it seemed an emerald flame, glowing with leaping green light. Her arms reached up and light poured from her long pointed fingers, weaving patterns in the air like lasers. She shook out her hair with the electric crackle of static and sparks flew in blinding white showers. The flames increased, moving around her, flaring blue and green; but they gave no heat, no hint of warmth, although the air was consumed with pale fire.

## 13

'Kate, wait! Where are we going?' Lisa tried to stop, but Davey's sister was holding her arm, pulling her through the crowd towards the bridge.

'Up there. Do you see that girl in the Victorian dress?' Kate pointed up towards where Elizabeth was waiting for them at the top of the steps. 'She wants to talk to you about Davey.'

Lisa had seen the girl before. She recognised her long thick wavy hair, the heart-shaped face, the immaculate Victorian dress. It was the girl who had been with Davey in the museum garden.

'What about Davey?' Lisa asked as she followed Kate up the steps. 'Where is he?'

For a second the world seemed to slow. Kate tripped, losing her footing at the second turn of the stairs. She fell forward, letting go of Lisa's arm to clutch on to the railing and save herself. When she turned back, her blue eyes were strange, unfocused, as though she had just woken from sleep.

'Who's Davey?' she replied, her voice was slurred, dreamy and deep.

Lisa stared at her, grey eyes wide. 'Davey is your brother.'

'You must be mistaken,' Kate replied with a puzzled smile, her voice returning to normal. 'I don't have a brother.'

'Come off it, Kate! Stop messing about!'

'I'm not.' Kate squinted down at her. 'Who are you, anyway?'

'I'm Lisa! Lisa Wilson! I'm in Davey's class at school . . .' Lisa broke off in confusion, disconcerted by the way the older girl was looking at her. She stepped away, stumbling backwards on the steps. Her skin prickled and the hairs were rising on the back of her neck. Something strange was happening here.

'Do you go to Wesson Heath Juniors?'

Lisa nodded.

'I can't say I've seen you around . . . And like I said, I don't have a brother.' Kate flicked her long fair hair out of her eyes. 'Ask these two if you don't believe me.' Her cousins had come down the steps to meet her. 'Tom, Elinor, meet – what did you say your name is again?'

'Lisa.'

'Meet Lisa. Now – do I have a brother?'

The twins both shook their heads and grinned. 'Not as far as *we* know.'

'I must have got mixed up . . .' Lisa backed away from them, thoroughly spooked.

'What was *that* all about?' Tom asked Kate as they clattered past and went off down the steps.

'Don't know,' Kate shrugged. 'Mistaken identity?'

'Must be . . . Where have you been, anyway?' Tom nodded to where the pageant was just starting. 'That looks *deeply* boring. I mean, what's the point of hanging around watching a bunch of kids we don't even know?'

Lisa stood on the platform halfway up the flight of steps, clinging on to the rails in front of her. She felt stunned and slightly sick, as though she had just received a sharp blow to the head. Why was Kate pretending not to know who she was? Lisa had been round at their house often enough. And why on earth would she say that she didn't have a brother? How could she say that? Lisa had known Davey since Nursery. They had started school together. They had been in the same class ever since. Lisa gripped the rail harder to keep her hands from trembling. Now Kate was talking as if no such person existed.

'Don't worry, Lisa.'

The voice in her ear was that of a stranger. Lisa started round. The hand on her shoulder had nearly made her jump out of her skin.

'Who are you?' The words came out husky, quavering.

'My name is Elizabeth. Kate was bringing you to me.'

'Yes. I remember. But then . . .' Lisa looked down, staring in panic to where Kate and her cousins had disappeared into the crowd.

'Shh.' Elizabeth squeezed the girl's shoulder, trying to calm her. 'Never mind that now. There's something I have to tell you.'

'Is it to do with Davey?'

'Yes.'

'So you don't think – don't think he—' Lisa bit her lip.

'Think he doesn't exist? No.' Elizabeth shook her head. 'I don't think that at all.'

'You were with him. That day at the museum. I've seen you before.'

'That's right.'

'Afterwards, Davey said you weren't there.'

'He was afraid you wouldn't believe him.'

'Because . . .' Lisa paused, she was having trouble saying the words, 'because you are a ghost?'

'That's right.'

'Oh, no.' Lisa pulled away, shaking her head in violent denial. 'Oh, no, no, no!'

'Lisa!' Elizabeth held the girl by the shoulders. 'I know you're frightened, and I know why, and it's all right. Someone came to you the other night, didn't they?'

'Yes.' Lisa was crying, sobbing with fear and confusion. 'My – my Gramps.'

'He has visited you before, hasn't he?'

'Yes. When I was very little.' She swallowed her tears and looked at Elizabeth. 'How do you know—?'

'The first time he came because you were very dear to him. The second time was to ask you something.'

'Ask me what?'

'To help stop Davey from being here tonight.'

78

'And I wouldn't listen.' Lisa's eyes grew wide with shock. 'It's all my fault . . .'

'No, Lisa. You mustn't think that. It's not just to do with you, what you did or didn't do. Davey would have ended up here anyway. No force on earth could have prevented it.' She paused for a moment, glancing up at the ghost crew ranged above her. The Blind Fiddler nodded slightly, urging her on. 'Tell me, Lisa. What was your mother's name before she was married?'

'Hamilton, Janet Hamilton . . .'

'My name is Hamilton, too.'

'I still don't see . . .' Lisa frowned, unsure where this was leading now.

'I want you to look at me. Look carefully. What do you see?'

'A girl, about my age, with long dark hair, dressed in Victorian clothes . . .'

'What else? What else do you see?'

Lisa looked into the heart-shaped face, the grey eyes set wide under strong black brows, the straight slightly snubbed nose, the full mouth, the firm chin with the slight cleft. Stubborn, Dad called it. Then she saw . . . If this girl's hair was cut short, or she wore hers longer . . . Lisa gasped as realisation struck her. She might as well have been looking into a mirror.

'Who are you?' she whispered.

'Your—' Elizabeth stopped to think for a moment. 'Your great great aunt by my calculation. Your grandfather was my brother Harry's son. I died when Harry was quite a little boy.'

Suddenly Lisa felt rather faint. 'Family stories. I've heard them talk— You were killed in an accident, involving a car, or something?'

'Yes. So *now* do you believe me?'

'Yes,' Lisa said quietly. 'I believe you. Where is Davey? Do you know?'

Elizabeth nodded. 'He is in the most terrible danger and only you can help him. I must, however, warn you that by going after him you put yourself at risk.'

How much, and in what way, Elizabeth did not have time to explain. She had asked the Fiddler's advice about this. The girl had a right to know, after all. In the end they had decided against a full explanation. It might seem callous, but to tell all might cause the girl to change her mind and that would jeopardise the entire enterprise.

Lisa did not think about the personal danger to herself. She hesitated for only a moment before asking,

'What do you want me to do?'

## 14

Davey was alone. There was no sign of the Lady. Her long drawn-out cry had turned into a siren wailing and then the world was burning. Not with cold blue fire. These flames roared and leapt, yellow, orange and red.

The War Memorial and the Peace Garden had disappeared. Tall buildings had grown up on every side, all along the street in which he found himself. He stood, trying to get his bearings, trying to work out what on earth was happening, while all around him timbers groaned, and walls collapsed.

The whole side of a building fell away with a terrible rending crash. Bricks avalanched down, sending up choking clouds of dust and smoke. It was like the museum's *Blitz Experience*, except he was *inside* the glass box . . .

Flames shot up showering sparks in all directions. Some hit Davey, peppering his white shirt with black dots, burning through to the skin. Davey felt panic surge through him. This was real. He had to get out of here. The heat was unbearable. It was like standing in the middle of a furnace.

He turned, desperately looking up and down, seeking the best means of escape. Either side of him, the street was a tunnel of curling flame. Nothing could exist here, he thought, no other creature.

Then he saw a small dark figure, etched against the terrible glare. Davey ran towards it, not caring if it was alive or ghost, friend or foe.

'Lisa!' Davey stood transfixed, staring at his friend. Of all the strange things that had happened so far, this was the strangest. 'How did you get here?'

'Elizabeth sent me,' Lisa explained simply. 'She said I was the only one who could help you. She said—' Lisa broke off as another building collapsed, showering burning debris as it fell in on itself with a groaning boom. She looked round, petrified. 'But if, I'd known, if I'd known . . .' Her voice trembled and stopped and she focused back on him again, red flames leaping in her grey eyes.

'It'll be all right, Lisa,' Davey said, putting his arm round her, trying to hide his own terror. 'We'll get out of here, just you wait and see. The important thing is we're together. There has to be a reason for that.'

They were lost in chaos, in a world where the normal rules did not apply. The Lady had warped the strands of fate and time, weaving them to her own ends. What these were, Davey could not guess, but he was beginning to understand: nothing happened to no purpose. Lisa being here had a meaning, but what it was, he did not know.

From some distance away came the urgent ringing of fire engines speeding to put out the blazes begun by the first wave of incendiary bombs. Davey and Lisa dodged down a side street, heading towards the sound. They left the tall warehouses and entered streets packed with darkened shops and houses. Fire rained down from the sky, catching in roofs and gutters, exploding in gardens, fizzing and flaring in blinding magnesium brightness. Firemen, wardens and volunteers dashed from one place to another; seeking to contain fires already started, trying to put out the incendiary devices before their flames took hold.

'Oi, you kids – what do you think you're doing?'

Lisa and Davey looked up to see a man dressed in uniform shouting at them and waving his arms. He wore a black tin hat with a white 'W' painted on the front of it. He was an air-raid warden, Davey knew that from History lessons.

'Stop!' he shouted, and came hurrying towards them, dodging potholes, and stepping over debris. 'There's a raid on, or haven't you noticed? What are you two doing out here? You should be down in the shelters.'

He stood before them, waiting for an answer, a squat, square-built man. His clothes were thick with dust. His knuckles were torn, his hands bleeding. Soot smeared his broad face which was etched deep with lines of tension and fatigue.

'We—' Davey started. 'I—' He tried to go on but his mouth was dry. He could find no words to describe their predicament, or his fear.

The planes were droning in, wave after wave of them, stitching bombs across the city. Incendiaries whistled and screamed down while anti-aircraft guns set up an incessant chatter of fire. Shrapnel and spent shells rattled and pattered on the roofs all around. From the distance came the thud and thump of high explosives. Lisa just stared, eyes stretched wide with terror, hands covering her ears.

The warden looked down at these children in front of him and his kind face creased in compassion. He had kids of his own, but they were all grown up. Jimmy was married with a kid now, young Sylvie. He was off fighting with the RAF; Jimmy could be up there right now, but it didn't seem yesterday that he was the age of these two here.

He looked them over, trying to assess the state they were in. No physical injuries that he could see, but they were both suffering from shock – that much was clear. Eyes stretched wide, skin pale and sweating, he doubted that he would get much sense out of them until this lot was over. The raid had come on so suddenly that they could have easily been caught outside playing and run the wrong way in all the confusion. It happened often. There would be time to sort it out in the morning. If any of them saw morning. He looked up at the burning sky, at the enemy planes caught like black specks in the walking fingers of searchlights. Tonight was going to be bad, he had a feeling about it. This would be the worst one yet.

'Come on,' he smiled down at the two children. 'We'd better get you to—'

He stopped speaking. Near, very near came the scream

of a bomb falling, then it ceased. He threw himself to the ground, an arm round either child. There was a flash of light and it was as if a great wind tore over them, dragging at the clothes on their bodies, seeking to wrench the hair from their heads. The road beneath them seemed to buckle, rolling like a shaken carpet, and it seemed as if some great force was trying to steal the very air that they were breathing, sucking it up into itself. Then came the most deafening explosion, loud enough to take away all hearing. Earth fountained and fell all over them, half burying their bodies in dirt and debris.

'We have to get out of here before the next lot comes over.'

The warden pulled them to their feet and set off at a run, dragging both of the children with him. Smoke and dust swirled in choking clouds as they careered down the street, avoiding craters, keeping away from the shattered houses. Whole walls had been pulled away, leaving ragged lines of brickwork around rooms spilling furniture. Bricks lay everywhere, piled up like discarded lego. Slates rivered down from broken roofs, wallpaper flapped above stairs zigzagging to nowhere. There was an unexploded bomb on the corner. He slowed, tiptoeing past it. In the next street was Public Shelter No. 6. It was a deep shelter. The children would be safe there.

They had to make a run for it before the next attack. He could hear the low rumble of bombers coming nearer, the howl of bombs descending, the steady thump and crump as the planes rained high explosive destruction down on the city he loved.

They set off again and Davey ran, his feet skidding and slipping on debris and rubble, trying to keep up as the man dragged him along. Then something sharp and metal bit into his shin and he had to stop. He thought it was shrapnel, from a shell or bomb casing. When he looked down his leg was bleeding. Near his foot lay a street sign. Twisted and bent by the blast, it was still possible to read the name by the lurid glow of fire and the eerie gleam of moonlight. The chipped enamel letters read: *Chapel Street*.

'What's your name?' Davey asked, his lips trembling.

'Harry,' the man replied. 'Harry Hamilton.'

# 15

'It's all right, son.' Harry bent to examine Davey's cut. 'It's just a scratch, nothing much. There will be worse if you don't get to the shelter. It's just up here.' He renewed his grip on their hands. 'Not far now.'

'No.' Davey pulled back, shaking his head, looking at Lisa. 'We can't go.'

'You have to,' Harry said gently. 'If you're worried about your mum and dad, we'll find them in the morning. They'd want you to be safe . . .'

Davey shook his head. 'It's not that. It's . . .' He stared at the man, unable to find the right words of warning. It was impossible to describe the terrible feeling inside him. He just stared, dark eyes huge in his chalk-white, dirt-streaked face.

Harry looked at him, puzzled, trying to understand what the youngster was going through. The boy seemed to be struggling with some terrible emotion, trying to deal with extremes too great for him. It was not surprising. To be out on a night like this, surrounded by fire and death and destruction, it was enough to test the bravest. He knew grown men who had been reduced to trembling hysteria, who had curled into balls and wept like babies. He ducked, pulling the children to him as more bombs

87

whistled and exploded around them. It was enough to put the fear of God into anyone, let alone a kid. But the raid was building in intensity. If they stayed out in the open, out in the street with no protection, they would all be killed.

'Come on, old chap.' He put his arm round Davey's shoulder, his voice low and reassuring. 'The shelter's just over here. You'll be safe in there. My daughter-in-law's down there, my Jimmy's wife Sarah with their baby, little Sylvie. Sarah'll look after you, she might even be able to rustle up a cup of tea . . .'

He was talking softly, chatting away, trying to sound as normal as possible, with one arm round both children, guiding their reluctant steps, when again they halted. This time it was the girl.

'We can't go.' The words came out flat. Matter-of-fact. At the sound of her grandparents' names, Lisa found her voice.

'We must—' Harry began to say, when he stopped. The girl was looking up at him. The grey eyes staring into his were no longer blank with fear. The look was sharp, intelligent, compelling attention.

'Listen, Harry.' The voice, although light as a child's, was not that of a frightened little girl. It held the calm gravity of one who had seen many years. 'Listen. You must listen to me.'

Harry nodded, obedient. He was not sure if the words came from this girl's mouth, or he heard them in his own head, but he knew the voice at once. It was Elizabeth. He remembered it well, and not just from life. He had never told anyone, but she came to him sometimes, appearing to him, too real to be a dream. He looked down at Lisa and saw his own sister: the eyes, the hair, the shape to the face . . .

'You must get everyone out of that shelter.'

'But—'

'Don't argue. There is no time. You must evacuate all the people and take them to another place. Get them out of Chapel Street. The shelter will suffer a direct hit. A bomb will fall through the upper storeys of the building above, detonating above the basement. It will bring the building down on top of the shelter, filling it with choking smoke and dust, blocking every exit, rupturing the water and gas mains and sewage pipes. The contents of these will pour down, drowning and suffocating any who might have survived. This will be among the worst bombing tragedies the city will suffer. All will be killed, including you, your daughter-in-law and your grandchild, and these children here. You must get the people out of there now. Do you understand?'

Harry nodded.

'Will you do it?'

Harry nodded again. Her word was enough. He needed no more to convince him.

'Very well. Go now. Do it quickly. And Harry?'

He turned back.

'Goodbye.'

His sister smiled. A tear streaked down his soot-stained cheek. They both knew that he would never see her in life again.

Davey stared in wonder at Lisa's cool authority, at the way the man was listening to what she was telling him. He stayed quiet and still, not daring to interrupt, offering up silent prayers of thanks. Somehow Elizabeth was speaking through Lisa, reaching out to defeat the Lady and save them all.

Harry jolted back into life. Bombs still screamed down all around them, but he did not hesitate. He rushed to the shelter, ordering the people out in batches, directing them to another shelter. Others gathered to help him with the work: police, wardens, and volunteers. The evacuation took time and demanded his full attention. When all the people were safe, he turned to thank his child companions, but they had disappeared.

## 16

Lisa and Davey were back in their own time, standing in the glimmering quietness of the Peace Garden. All the noise, the chaos and confusion had gone. They were in front of the white stone memorial. It seemed just as before, as though nothing had happened. The marble slab still carried its long, sad catalogue of names, but the area at the base, the part which the Lady had showed him, the memorial to Harry and those who died in the Chapel Street Shelter, that had gone. Davey knelt down to part the grass growing at the base. There was no sign, no reference, it was as if the carved letters had been erased.

He pointed it out to Lisa, explaining to her how the Lady had brought him here.

'Harry was my great grandfather.' Lisa spoke, her voice low and trembling. 'Hamilton is my mum's maiden name. That was my grandmother down in the shelter, along with my Aunt Sylvie.'

'So how—'

'Elizabeth, your ghost friend, is – was Harry's sister. In the garden, at the museum, she saw that I looked like her, that there is a connection between us. When she worked out what the Lady had planned, she saw it meant danger to me, as well as to you, but it gave her an idea.' She frowned. 'I don't really understand how, but the connection meant that she could use me to enter the banned part of the city. She was hoping that Harry would recognise the similarity, and then she could speak to him through me, kind of like a medium. He would listen to her and do what she said about getting the people out of the shelter. And it worked, thank goodness.'

'If the Lady had succeeded . . .' Davey's eyes grew wide at the full horror of what had been planned for him.

'You would have died there. After she took you, even Kate forgot that you existed. And I would never have been born. Come on, Davey,' Lisa shivered as the enormity of what might have happened closed in on her. 'Let's get out of here.'

From behind them came a series of screaming shrieks and deafening explosions. Davey leapt round, ready to throw himself to the ground. He grabbed hold of Lisa, to drag her down with him, but she was laughing.

'It's all right Davey, it's only fireworks.'

She pointed down to the river. Red, gold and green lights trembled in the dark reflecting water.

'We're safe, Davey.' She laughed again, and hugged him to her. 'We're safe!'

They watched together as rocket after rocket soared over the city to explode in the velvet night sky. The fireworks were a traditional part of the Victorian Evening, they heralded the Grand Parade, led by Father Christmas's Sleigh. But when everyone else saw the grand finale, Santa waving 'Merry Christmas'; Davey saw the Lady's face in the shimmering lights. She looked down on him, her crimson mouth smiling, her white hair an exploding mass of stars trailing light. The jewel on her forehead sparked red above wide slanting eyes which glittered silver and green.

'*So you cheat me once again, Davey Williams, you and your ghost friends. But remember this: the child born within the chimes of midnight is ever unlucky. I will come again. And the third time I come for you, there will be no escaping. I will come by ways unexpected, and do not look for help from either living or dead.*'

Davey turned, face clay-white under the play of multi-coloured lights.

'Did you see that?' he asked urgently. 'Did you see her? Did you hear what she said?'

'See what, Davey?' Lisa looked at him curiously. 'I just saw Santa. He was waving, wishing everybody Happy Christmas over the tannoy system, just like he does every year. Come on.'

She pulled at his arm, but he stayed rooted to the spot, staring up at the sky. The last of the rockets hovered, exploding above them like a supernova, before falling into the Old Town, leaving behind it a long train of trailing stars.

# 17

'Where have you two been?'

The second half of the pageant had begun and Kate had been sent to look for them. She'd looked everywhere, and had almost given up. Now they came strolling out of the darkness as if they had all the time in the world.

'That Miss Malkin's going crazy and Craddock's doing his nut.'

Davey flinched at the sound of the name the Lady had adopted. All his terror came back to him. The vision in the sky had been mocking him; she was playing with him again. She had been here all the while, biding her time, waiting for him. They had not escaped at all. He held Lisa's hand tightly and would have bolted, taking her with him, except for a hand grabbing him and a voice shouting, 'Not so fast!'

He turned to see a pale, sharp-featured young woman scowling down at him. She would have been pretty, except for the anger distorting her features. Her pale eyes gleamed from slanted slits above high cheek bones, her fine nostrils flared and her scarlet mouth was clamped in a thin line. Her cheap alloy headdress was slightly askew and the shiny green material of her long dress creased and rumpled. She had none of the terror and majesty of the

Lady. She was just an ordinary person. The spirit who had possessed her had gone. Davey relaxed in the face of her anger. Human fury – he could deal with that. The Lady had departed – for now.

'Where have you been?'

'We – we went to look at something – and – and we kind of got lost. We're really sorry—'

'Yes, sorry, Miss Malkin,' Lisa joined Davey in a stumbling litany of apology.

'Come on! I haven't got time to listen to you two snivelling and whining excuses. We've had our turn put back twice already. I'll have words to say to you two afterwards.'

She swept off in the direction of the performance area with Davey and Lisa following meekly along in her wake.

## 18

The play went well. Everyone cheered and applauded as Wesson Heath Juniors acted out the Mummers' ancient ritual story. The sword dance was particularly well received, the crowd reacting with a satisfying intake of breath as Davey sank to his knees. It was such a success, in fact, that Mr Craddock and Miss Malkin forgot their anger and congratulated Davey and Lisa along with everybody else.

Afterwards Lisa joined Davey and his family to celebrate his birthday. The Victorian Evening was in full swing. Davey's dad gave them money to spend on anything they wanted: old-fashioned fairground rides, sideshows and coconut stalls, paper bags of sticky sweets, baked potatoes and cones of hot chestnuts. Eventually Lisa and the Williams family went home along with all the other people, leaving the city to its past and its ghosts.

Jack, Polly, Elizabeth, and the others had stayed to watch over their friends, blending in with the living. Now they left too, returning across the dark river to the world of the dead. As they crossed the bridge, their mood became more sombre. Tall cranes and swinging jibs reached up into the night sky, signalling change coming to their part of the city. Change meant trouble. They did not know yet where the trouble might be coming from, or what it might mean for them. They did not even know if they could deal with it themselves. It could well be beyond their power. If that was the case then they might need the help of their human friends. After all, one good turn deserves another.

# Easter

# 1

Davey felt the familiar shiver, the old prickling of the skin, as he crossed over the bridge to the old part of the city. An odd tingling sensation spread up his spine and down to his fingers. Premonition. A mixture of fear and anticipation. Something was going to happen. He wondered if his companions were feeling anything. Kate, his sister, was up ahead, nearly at Cannongate which marked the entrance to the Old Town. His cousins, Tom and Elinor, were wandering along some way behind, chatting away, relaxed and happy. So it's only me, Davey thought. He'd had such premonitions before, but he tried to put this one out of his mind. He didn't want to spoil the afternoon for them all.

They were on their way to visit an archaeological dig that was going on somewhere near the cathedral. It was Kate's pet project. She'd been on about it for weeks. Mr Watson, her History teacher, had asked if any of the class would like to come along and join the Riverside Rescue Dig during the Easter holidays. Kate had taken this as a personal invite. Tom and Elinor were keen, too. It would be something interesting to do during their stay with Davey and Kate. Davey *had* been looking forward to it. It was only now that he felt a twinge of doubt.

101

He had not been into the city centre since the New Year, and, as he crossed the bridge, he deliberately did not look down at the Memorial Gardens that stretched along the river. He didn't want to think about what had happened there at Christmas. He kept his eyes forward. Ahead lay the Old Town. The site of the midsummer Haunts Tour. What had happened there, had happened to all of them: him, Kate, Elinor and Tom. They had stumbled into another city, one full of ghosts and spirits, existing beneath the surface of the one they knew. Davey stopped, testing the air around him, but he could sense nothing. The air seemed neutral, the world as solid as usual. His sister and cousins up ahead showed no signs of apprehension, no prickling premonition as they stood laughing together in the spring sunshine, gazing down at the glittering river, waiting for him to catch up.

The mild day had certainly brought out the tourists. Other groups were making their way through Cannongate, the ancient stone gateway into the city. They looked round as they entered the walls of the Old Town, talking excitedly, deciding on places to visit. They returned every year, coming back with the spring like migrating birds.

High above, the cathedral clock struck the hour, making Davey jump. He pushed back his dark brown hair, telling himself not to be stupid. No one else was feeling anything and nothing could happen at two o'clock on a March afternoon, could it?

To the right of them was a huge hoarding showing an

idealised view of the proposed Riverside Development: *A combined project of conversion and renewal, blending past and present, leading the city forward into the new millennium.* The work had started just before Christmas and was set to continue for many months. It took in an extensive area stretching from behind the cathedral down to the river. Temporary buildings, erected after the last war, were being cleared away. Other buildings, warehouses and stores, derelict for years, were being restored and converted. Public spaces, grassed over and concreted, were to be utilised more effectively. There was going to be a new Visitors' Centre and an old ship's chandler was to be made into a maritime museum. There would be shops and cafés all along the riverside, as well as low-rise housing, a craft centre and a new arts complex.

It might be nice when it was finished, Davey thought, as he stared up at the pictures of smart people wearing sunglasses and drinking cappuccinos. *If* it was ever finished. Davey looked down to the place where the work was going on, to the place where they were heading. It looked like one huge building site. The whole area was a sea of mud.

Wire fences sagged round a series of giant holes in the ground. Cranes reached up into the sky. Diggers, JCBs, every conceivable kind of earth-moving equipment littered the ground. The tourists turned away, this was not what they had come to see. They took off in search of the unspoilt areas that still kept the illusion of timelessness for which the city was famous.

'Good thing we're wearing wellies,' Ellie said with a wry grin as they set off. Kate was already picking her way through the squelching clay.

'How are we supposed to find them among all this lot?' Tom asked, when they caught up with Kate.

'Well, er . . .' Kate bit her lip. The scene was not quite what she had imagined.

'We could ask that bloke over there.' Davey pointed to a burly man leaning against a fence. 'He doesn't seem to be doing much.'

Nor did anybody else. Men stood around in bunches, or sat on any available surface. Work seemed to have stopped.

Kate approached the man who had his hard hat pushed back and his arms folded. The material of his check shirt stretched tight across his broad chest, his mud-encrusted jeans sagging down beneath his ample stomach.

'Excuse me,' she said. 'We're looking for the conservation dig.'

'You mean that archaeology bird from the museum and her mob?'

Kate nodded.

He jerked his thumb. 'Over there someplace. You'll be able to spot 'em.' He gave a humourless laugh. 'They'll be the only ones working.'

'Oh?' Tom asked. 'Why's that?'

'A hold up.' His broad brow clenched under his plastic helmet. 'Been one thing after another. If it's not them archaeologists having to check out every little thing we turn up, it's accidents. Nothing big, minor mostly, but enough to stop, and time mounts up. Or it's plant playing up, engines stopping, generators cutting out. We're weeks behind target, and the project's only just started. If I didn't know better, I'd say we was jinxed.' This time he followed his humourless laugh by spitting on the ground.

Davey looked up sharply at the mention of this last word. He noticed several of the men in the vicinity do the same thing.

'Look at 'em! Jittery as a pack of Brownies. Muttering and whispering about ghosts and gremlins. Too many lunchtime pints more likely.'

'Where did you say they were, exactly?' Kate asked again.

'Over there someplace, like I said.' He squinted down, his beefy face creased with disapproval. 'You shouldn't even be here, strictly speaking. This is a hard hat area. It's a construction site, not an adventure playground.'

'We aren't trespassing,' Kate explained. 'We've been invited on the dig. We've got permission . . .'

She faltered, worried that he was going to throw them out altogether.

'All right, love,' he said, softening slightly. 'I'll get one of my lads to take you there. Mick!' He shouted to the group lounging nearest to them. 'Over here!'

A young man detached himself and ambled over.

'Take these to that archaeology mob and don't get lost

yourself.' Nearby a generator juddered into action. 'Hey up. We're on again. Shape yourselves, you lot!'

'Don't take no notice,' Mick said as he guided them through the different parts of the site. 'The gaffer's all right really, heart's in the right place. He just gets narky like, when work stops. The people you're looking for are over there.' He indicated a marked-off area where several people were squatting down, scraping away close to the ground. 'Get them to give you hard hats. I'm serious!' He pushed his own helmet back. 'Whatever the gaffer says, there's a lot think this job's jinxed. Men are leaving because of it. It's not just the accidents and plant cutting out. You'd expect that. Some have heard things, seen things . . .'

'Like what?' Davey asked, his curiosity aroused again.

'Difficult to say straight out,' the young man rubbed his arms. Goosebumps appeared on his skin's surface. 'Sounds silly when you say it out loud. You kind of have to be there. But . . . I've got a mate, right? On security, works nights. He *swears* there's something weird happening. He's reckoned to be a bit of a hard man, doesn't scare easy, like, but he says some nights out here would be enough to spook anybody. I'm telling you . . .' He shivered again and looked round warily, as if others might be listening. 'This place is jinxed.'

## 2

Davey followed the others, plodding through the mud towards yet another fenced-off area. Inside the wire enclosure, a central trench had been dug and widened into a pit several metres square. People were working on their hands and knees, painstakingly scraping away with small trowels, stopping every now and then to examine a find and put it to one side, marking the place with a little sticker, before starting on the next square inch. Others were riddling piles of spoil, picking things out, washing them in buckets before placing them on a rickety table erected in one corner.

They were all so absorbed that the children approached unobserved. Kate was anxiously scanning the squatting figures, looking for Mr Watson, her History teacher. He was the real reason that they were here. Personally, Davey was sick of hearing about him. It had been 'Mr Watson thinks this . . .', and 'Mr Watson says that . . .', ever since she'd started in his class at the beginning of the year. He was the reason she had suddenly stopped wanting to be a vet and now wanted to be an historian or an archaeologist.

'Which one *is* he?' Tom asked Davey.

'That one over there, I think.' Davey grinned suddenly. 'Kate fancies him.'

'I heard that!' Kate whirled round as the two boys laughed. 'I do not!'

Her indignation just made Davey and Tom laugh harder. They could both see that she was blushing.

'Don't take any notice,' Elinor said to Kate. 'They can't help being stupid. They're only boys.'

'Hey! Who are you calling stupid?' Tom made to grab his sister.

'Stop it, for goodness' sake!' Kate was desperate not to be shown up. 'He's seen us!'

A tall man in his early twenties, dressed in pale-coloured cords and a denim shirt, was coming towards them.

'Kate! How nice to see you!' His smile showed immaculate white teeth. He took off his hard hat and thick locks of fair floppy hair fell into his dark blue eyes. 'And these are?'

Kate introduced her brother and cousins.

'Welcome!' He smiled again and even Davey had to admit that he was good-looking. 'Come over here and meet the gang. Then we'll kit you out and you can get stuck in.' They wandered over to the rest of the team.

'This is Mari. Dr Mari Jones.' Mr Watson introduced a tall serious-looking young woman dressed in work boots, combat pants and a grey T-shirt. 'She's in charge here.'

'Hi.' She brushed her palms on the seat of her trousers. 'I won't shake hands.' A grin broke her rather stern expression. 'Mine are filthy. Richard said to expect

108

visitors.' Her smile widened, spreading to green eyes flecked with brown. She took off her helmet, shaking out her shiny auburn hair. Her fair skin was beginning to freckle from working outdoors in the spring sunshine. 'More the merrier. Now, let me explain what's going on here.'

She frowned again and gazed down to where her co-workers were crawling around like beetles. To Davey, the whole area just looked like a patch of mud with stickers on it.

'What you see here is one corner of one part of a huge Benedictine monastery, known as the Priory. It extended from the cathedral, right down to the river.'

'Phew.' Davey stared around. 'It must have been massive. Where did all it go?'

'There's very little left now, apart from the cathedral church, of course. It was subject to a series of scandals and suppressed at the time of the Reformation in the reign of Henry VIII. The monks dispersed and the land and buildings were seized by the Crown. All that's left is what you see here.' She pointed at the lumps of stone they were working around. 'But we've got a pretty good idea of what it was like and how extensive it was from old plans and drawings as well as inventories and written descriptions.'

'What's this bit here?' Kate asked, looking down into the muddy pit.

'Well, Kate,' Mr Watson took over, 'we think this is

part of a cloister. The inner wall runs along here and we've found a doorway over there that leads into another room, possibly the chapter house, which would have been the administrative and disciplinary centre of the monastery, where the monks would meet . . .'

As he talked on, Davey tried to imagine a whole complex of buildings, with monks hurrying round. If it covered the area that Dr Jones said, it must have been as big as a small village.

'Aren't you worried about all this building work going on and disturbing everything?' he asked her.

'Oh, no. It gives us a chance to get in and see what's here. This is the first dig in the old part of the city for some time. If we find anything really interesting, they will preserve it and incorporate it into the new Visitors' Centre. Do you want to see what we've found so far today?'

'Sure.' Davey nodded.

'All right. Come this way.' She led them to the table in the corner. 'We collect here each day and remove the things each night to the City Museum for conservation and safe-keeping.'

'What's that?' Tom pointed in between the fragments of pottery and tile to what looked like a little squashed bottle.

'It's a pilgrim's ampulla. Used to carry holy water. There's a pilgrim's badge next to it. Pilgrims collected things like these as souvenirs – rather like you might buy a hat with Blackpool on it – to show where they had visited. They were probably dropped by someone going to or coming from the shrine of St Wulfric.'

'Where was that?'

'In the cathedral.'

'Who was St Wulfric?' Davey asked. 'How come he had a shrine and everything?'

'He founded the first church here way back in the seventh century and he was the first bishop. He was also martyred and a shrine grew up in the place where he was killed. Of course, it was just a little church, then, not much more than a collection of hermits' cells—'

'Mari? Can you come over here for a minute?' one of her helpers interrupted.

'Excuse me.' Mari turned to see what he wanted. 'I'll have to leave you with Richard.'

'Mr Watson—' Kate began as Mari left them.

'Call me Richard,' the teacher smiled. 'It *is* the holidays and we're not in school, after all.'

Davey raised an eyebrow. He couldn't imagine doing that to his own teacher, Mr Craddock. He didn't even know Craddock's first name, come to think of it. He probably didn't have one. It probably said 'Mr' on his birth certificate.

Richard showed them some more of the finds made that day, including a couple of seals, a ring and a bit of a bronze bell. The objects were black with corrosion, but the children could feel the excitement of discovery tug at them. These things were at least four hundred years old. It was interesting, thinking who might have dropped them, who might have owned them. So when Richard suggested that they might like to have a go themselves, they were all for it.

The teacher gave out trowels and hard hats. These had to be worn for Health and Safety reasons, he explained. Davey's was too big for him. It came down over his ears, lodging on his eyebrows. He peered out, determined to take it off at the first opportunity. What was supposed to fall on him? The only thing above them was the sky.

The four children clustered at Richard's end of the trench, trowels in hand, while he showed them how to scrape carefully at the ground, looking for anything in the slightest way unusual. Even a difference in texture or shade in the sticky red clay could be significant.

'If you find something, call me or one of the others. We'll help you get it out. You never know how deep it is in. Also age and the dampness of the earth makes even normally hard material like metal or wood extremely fragile, easily damaged.'

Davey was fidgeting by now, desperate to have a go, but before that could happen, Mari interrupted them.

'Richard, can you come here a second?' she called from the other end of the trench. 'Listen to this.'

One of her helpers had uncovered a stone slab and was rapping on it with the handle of his trowel. Richard went over, followed by Kate, Tom and Elinor. Davey stayed where he was, thinking to have a quiet little dig on his own. He squatted down, studying the ground. Suddenly he was aware of a strange hollow booming sound. Cracks began appearing beneath his feet. He looked up sharply. Richard was jumping up and down, saying, 'I think you're right. There's a space under here.'

Richard was a big man. Tall and heavy. Mari was shouting at him, telling him to stop, when there was a rending, tearing crash and Davey disappeared.

# 3

It was a good thing, after all, that he had been wearing his hard hat. Davey tumbled into space and then bounced down followed by a showering fall of stones and rubble. He came to rest at the bottom of a wide flight of steps. He flung his arms up instinctively, trying to ward off the falling earth, but a chunk of stone caught him a hard blow right on top of his helmet and for a minute the world blurred, shuddering around him. He sat in dazed confusion, waiting for his head to come right again, before looking around, blinking grit from his eyes, peering into the dust-laden darkness. Light from the ragged hole above showed him to be in some kind of underground chamber. All around was blackness.

Just for an instant, only a second, it seemed that he was not alone. He was suddenly aware of something fluttering, a rustle in the corner, as of skin on skin, or leathery wings. Then it seemed as though something was looking up at him, tiny green sparks in the dark, like the eyes of an animal disturbed at its kill. It gave a hiss, and Davey was aware of a foul blast of air, and then, just as suddenly, it was gone. Davey shuddered, almost overwhelmed by a feeling of fear and nausea, but when he looked back there was nothing. I took a knock, Davey thought, maybe it's just the shock. He shook his head, hoping against hope that he had been hallucinating, because the thing he had seen was not from this world.

He heard voices from above, people asking if he was all right. He looked up to see anxious faces peering down at him. He stood up, his knees feeling kind of wobbly, and climbed what was left of the crumbling steps. As he reached the top of the flight, arms stretched to meet him and pull him out into the light.

'And for my next trick . . .' he said shakily, cracking a joke to let them know that he was all right.

'What's down there?' Tom asked. 'Did you see anything?'

'No,' said Davey, a little too quickly.

Tom and Kate looked at each other, alerted by his tone of voice.

'Are you OK, Davey?' Elinor asked. Davey looked very pale and frightened. It could be just the fall, of course, but he looked as though he'd seen something – he had seen things, strange things, before.

'Well . . .' Davey began, dropping his voice to a whisper, but before he could say more Kate's teacher came over to see how he was.

Mr Watson was asking questions about whether he had hit his head or not and holding up fingers for him to count. Dr Jones was standing by as well, looking down at Davey, her arms folded, forehead creased in a frown.

'He really ought to go to hospital,' she said. 'This is my site. Any accidents, I'm responsible—'

'Oh, no!' Davey looked up at her, shocked and stricken. He did not like people fussing over him and he might miss something if he went now. Also Kate would have to go with him, and he could just imagine how she'd feel about that. Quite apart from anything else, Mum would go hysterical if they phoned her from the hospital. Davey shook his head. It hardly bore thinking about. 'I'm all right,' he said vehemently. 'Honest. I didn't hurt myself at all,' he lied. 'I only tumbled a little way.'

'Hmm.' The archaeologist's frown deepened, then her concerned face brightened. 'One of the volunteers is a doctor. I'd completely forgotten.' She looked up at Richard Watson. 'I could get her to check him over. See what she thinks.'

He nodded. 'Good idea.'

Davey waited in resignation as the doctor came hurrying over. He hated being the centre of attention and had almost convinced himself that he felt all right now.

The doctor came to look in Davey's eyes and ears and feel his bones. Davey endured her attention in an agony of impatience, watching the others disappear like rabbits into the hole he had found.

Dr Jones went first.

'The roof seems sound enough,' she said, when she came back up. 'It's a barrel construction. No way in. No way out. Except from above.' She held up a piece of rotten wood. 'Looks like there was some kind of trap door, covered with packed earth and then later surfaces. It rotted away and then waited for Davey to come and stand on it,' she added with a quick grin over at him.

'Can *we* go and have a look?' Tom asked her.

'I don't see why not,' she said with a shrug of her slim shoulders and let herself back down into the space.

The others followed, bringing what torches and lights they could find, leaving Davey on the surface to answer questions and wiggle his toes.

'What do you think it is?' Kate asked, looking round the underground chamber. It appeared to be empty.

'Who knows? Underground storage? Cellarage? Could even have been a dwelling. You know what the city's like, one level built on top of another.'

'Like Cairncross Close?' Kate asked. She had visited the city's most notorious underground site last midsummer. She shivered as the experience came back to her, brought on by the chill air and the cold stone smell.

'Yes, that's right.' The archaeologist looked surprised at the girl's knowledge. 'How did you know about that?'

'We went there last summer. On a Haunts Ghost Tour.'

'Ah.' The archaeologist nodded. 'I know. They finish their tours quite near here.'

'Could this join up with the same tunnels and underground passages?' Kate shivered again, remembering their own hair-raising journey through them; then glanced up quickly, hoping that her companion would put the shudder down to the drop in temperature underground.

'I don't think so. Much more likely to be part of the monastery. Although where one lot of passages start and others end, it's sometimes hard to say.'

'Mari. Over here.' One of her assistants beckoned from the far corner. 'I think this might be something.'

Kate went with her to see what they had found.

'What is it?' she asked as the archaeologist walked round, studying the slight rise in the floor.

'I'm not sure . . .'

Tom joined Kate. The stone slab they were staring at looked like all the others. He failed to see anything different about it.

'What's so special?' he asked.

'The markings, see?' Mari pointed to some scratches. She took out a piece of chalk from her pocket and rubbed it lightly across the stone surface. 'It's an *Agnus Dei*.'

'What's that?'

'It means, literally, the lamb of God. It shows a figure of a lamb bearing a cross or flag, in this case a cross. It's a symbol of Christ and also St John.' She scanned the rest of the floor. 'There's nothing else like it. All the other stones are blank.'

'Maybe it's medieval graffiti. Maybe someone was down here, one of the monks for instance, and scratched it on when he got bored.'

'Maybe. Or maybe it's some kind of marker—'

'Oh, like X marks the spot?' Tom was suddenly finding it much more interesting. 'Maybe there's something *underneath*, you mean?'

'Exactly.' The archaeologist grinned up at him and began picking at the uneven edge with a Swiss army knife. 'Worth a look, don't you think?' She stood up, dusting her hands on her combat pants. 'We'd better get some stuff down here to shift it and we need more light.'

Four people, each with a crowbar, levered the stone into a position where it could be moved out of the way. Mari Jones knelt down, torch in hand, peering into the hollow. Tom squatted down next to her, anxious to see. He sat back, disappointed. Underneath was just another grey slab. Another layer of floor.

Up above, after the doctor had finished looking him over, Davey went to the edge of the hole. He had been feeling distinctly left out, watching with mounting frustration as people scurried from every corner of the site, carrying heavy tools and more lights, taking them underground.

A minute ago he had been desperate to see what had been found but now he held back from looking down. Excited voices came up from below, calling instructions, making suggestions, countering question with question: 'What do you think we've got?', 'What do you think it is?'

Davey could feel their building anticipation, but his own foreboding was growing heavy, stifling like a blanket. He knelt down and looked in cautiously. The corner where they were working was where he had seen the 'thing'. He tried not to think about it; tried to convince himself that it had just been his imagination. Maybe he *had* hit his head, and then suffered a hallucination. But he did not really believe that. He had seen this thing before, or something very similar. It was a Sentinel, he was almost sure. Sentinels were ghastly supernatural creatures who wore flapping black robes around skeletal frames, and hoods to hide their skull-like faces. Sentinels were the guardians of the ghost city, feared by all who dwelt there. He had seen them last Midsummer's Eve. But that was in *their* world. What was one doing *here*, in the *real* world? What could it possibly be after? And how did he see it?

'You OK, mate?' Tom was looking up at him.

'Yeah. Fine,' Davey replied, although he didn't feel it. He was shivering now and his teeth were chattering.

'Want a hand down?' Tom offered a grubby paw.

'Sure.' Davey accepted Tom's help into the underground cavity. He did not want his cousin thinking he was some kind of wimp. 'Anything happening?'

'They found a kind of box thing,' Tom explained. 'That was exciting. But now they've got the lid off, there's just more floor. Could go on forever. Way she talked,' he nodded his sandy head towards the archaeologist, 'I thought they were going to find treasure— Hang on a minute.'

The archaeologist was lifting the grey slab now, but it looked kind of thin and floppy, not like stone at all . . .

'Hey, *that* looks more interesting.' Tom moved to rejoin them. 'You coming, Davey?'

Davey shook his head. What they were about to find meant trouble, big trouble, he knew with sudden and absolute certainty, but he could not speak. It was as if the jolting blow to the head had somehow sharpened his psychic awareness, taking it up to a level that left him shaking, feeling sick. His face was sweat-sheened, white in the darkness of the cellar. Freckles stood out, grey and brown, like mud spattered across his nose and cheeks. Tom came back to him, concerned, but Davey waved him away.

'I just feel a little dizzy, that's all,' he managed to mutter. 'Must be the fall. I'll be OK.'

Everyone was crowding round Dr Jones. Tom had to elbow to the front to see what all the fuss was about.

'What have they found?' he asked Elinor, who was kneeling over the opening.

'Bones. They've found bones, Tom. Just look.'

She moved so he could see. The bones were lying in a cist: a stone box. Tom peered into a slate-lined area a metre or more long and perhaps half a metre wide. Beneath a patchy web of rotted material, the bones were piled neatly into the compact space: long leg bones at the sides, skull nestling in between shorter arms and ribs. Whoever these bones belonged to certainly had not been buried there. The bones would not even have made up a whole skeleton; there seemed to be significant bits missing. Tom was not sure what bones looked like after they had been in the grave for long periods of time, but these were dark brown and glossy, almost as though they had been given a coat of furniture polish.

However old they were, and however they got here, one thing was sure. Whoever these bones belonged to must have suffered a violent death. The skull had been cracked open like an Easter egg. There was a whole chunk missing just above the forehead.

# 4

Tom, Kate and Elinor joined Davey near the entrance. They had been sidelined. The circle of intense activity centred round this new find was no place for amateurs.

Tom failed to see why they couldn't whip the whole lot out right away.

'Archaeologists don't work like that,' Kate said loftily. 'It's a painstaking business, to do with conservation and scholarship. The tiniest little scrap of material speaks volumes to the skilled eye. What they are doing now, for instance—'

'OK, OK.' Tom scowled his impatience. 'Spare me the lecture. What was that stuff they got out first, anyway? That over there?' He pointed to the grey–white slab of thin buckled material.

'Oh, it's a sheet of lead. It was lying over the bones. It's got writing on it. Latin they think, but it's very faint. They will have to take it back to the museum and have an expert take a look at it.'

'Why lead?' Elinor asked.

'I don't know.' Tom shrugged. 'Maybe he was radio-active.'

'What are they doing now?' Davey asked. Now the bones were actually revealed, he felt a little better.

'Taking all the itty bitty bits of fabric out with tweezers and putting them into special containers ready to be conserved. They are especially important.'

'Why?'

'Well.' Kate was enjoying her role as self-appointed expert. 'Because it's likely to be linen, or some organic material, and this makes it easy to calculate the age by carbon dating. When they've done that, they can say when he was put down there, and have a good guess by whom. It's like historical detective work. I find it fascinating—'

'But slow!' Tom complained. 'We could be here all the rest of the day watching people mess about with tweezers. If it doesn't liven up in a bit, I vote we go.' He looked round the others. 'We can always come back tomorrow.'

'Hmm, I guess.' Kate nodded.

Davey shook his head violently. 'No!'

'What's the matter, Davey?' Elinor asked gently. He had been very quiet ever since he'd come down here and he was still very pale. 'Did you hurt yourself in the fall?'

'No, it's not that.' He shook his head. He could not find the words to explain but what he was feeling went way past the physical. 'We have to stay until they take the bones away.'

'Are you *sure* you're all right?' Kate looked at her brother with new concern. He was looking very pasty and he was acting strangely, even for Davey. 'Maybe I'd better get you home,' she added. 'You could have concussion – like the time you were knocked down by that car—'

'Don't fuss, Kate. It's not that, all right?'

'Well, what is it, then?'

'I don't know. I'm not sure, not exactly. I – I can't explain it, but I just have this feeling – the bones must not stay here all night. They have to get them out of here,' Davey finished, his voice low and urgent.

'I don't understand.' Tom frowned. 'I mean, what difference does it make?'

'I'm not sure . . . I don't understand either, but it could make a big difference, a very big difference.' Davey's normally bright brown eyes became unfocused, dull and cloudy. 'All the difference in the world. I – I thought I saw something,' he added after a moment or two. 'You know, when I fell in. It was over in that corner.' Davey shuddered. 'Kind of hovering.' He dropped his voice again. 'It was a – a Sentinel. Just for an instant it was there. And before anyone says anything, I was *not* hallucinating. I saw it. It was real!'

Davey glared, daring them to disbelieve him. The others had seen Sentinels. They knew what they were. They had been through the same experiences. They had been in the ghost city. They all knew that it was possible to slip between worlds. Davey looked from one face to the another. The odd thing was that it seemed as though he was the only one who fully remembered. For the others, each time was like a brand new encounter; each time they had to be convinced all over again.

125

'What? Here?' Tom's forehead wrinkled in disbelief. 'In *this* world? You had to be dreaming, Davey.'

'Or it *could* be a blow to the head.' Kate's anxiety was genuine. She was deeply worried about him. 'Perhaps you really ought to go to the hospital, like Dr Jones said.'

'Or it could be, just might be, that he's telling the truth,' Elinor chipped in, rounding on her brother and cousin. 'What if he did see something? What if he actually saw what he said? You are always so quick to doubt him, to dismiss what he's saying. It was the same at Hallowe'en – but I'll tell you one thing – he's right more often than you two are.'

Davey shot her a look of thanks.

'OK, OK.' Kate nodded, point taken. Davey was more sensitive than the rest of them. She turned to him. 'Do you feel anything now?'

'No, but . . .'

'But what? We promise to listen.' Kate glanced over to Tom. 'Spit it out.'

'I've got a feeling . . .' Davey paused, making up his mind to tell them. 'It's about the bones. It *is* just a feeling. No.' He thought before going on. 'It's more than that. They must not stay here overnight.' He eyed the activity in the corner. 'And it looks like everyone's getting ready to pack up, so they just might.'

'Oh, right.' Kate thought she knew what was coming. 'And how are we supposed to guarantee that the bones are taken out?'

'You've got to tell them.'

'And they're going to take any notice?' Kate rolled her eyes. 'I don't think so, Davey.'

'You must—'

'Or?'

'Something terrible will happen.'

'Such as?'

'I don't know . . .' Davey shrugged. 'I just know it will, that's all.'

'But why me? Why not you?'

'Because you know Mr Watson.' Davey looked at her, his brown eyes pleading. 'And you're older. They're more likely to listen to you.'

'I'm still a kid, remember? Just like you.' Kate was nearly fourteen, and acted pretty grown up when it suited her. 'Anyway,' she added quickly, before Davey could point that out, 'he's not in charge, is he? I'd have to convince Dr Jones. There's no way she'd listen to me. Why should she?'

'I don't know,' Davey repeated, his conviction growing stronger every minute. 'I just know we've got to get the bones out of here . . .'

'That's brilliant!' Kate folded her arms. 'You want me to go over there and tell a load of adult experts what they should be doing. And why? Because my brother has a *feeling*—'

'There could be a way,' Elinor intervened. She trusted Davey's *feelings* much more than the other two did.

127

'Like what?' Kate turned to her cousin.

'Tell them it's for safe-keeping. Say that on the way over, a man was telling us about vandalism, interference. I mean, it's not lying, not strictly, and they obviously think the find is important, so they wouldn't want to risk anything happening to it . . .'

'Yeah,' Kate smiled, 'that might just work. You come with me. You can back me up.'

They went to join the group round the bones and Kate gave the thumbs up: mission accomplished. Not that she'd had anything to do with it. The archaeological team had no intention of leaving the find here overnight. Human remains had to be removed for safe-keeping, and the police and the Coroner's Office would have to be to be informed.

'Standard procedure,' Dr Jones explained. 'We were kind of expecting it. This is a church site, after all, we were bound to come across a grave or two.'

But not quite like this one, she thought, as she prepared to lift the skull and put it in the box brought in to receive it. She paused for a moment, looking down at the dark dome in its nest of bones. This was no conventional burial. These bones had been carefully placed here, concealed in this stone cist, deliberately hidden from the world. The smooth polished surface of the skull was like darkened alabaster, or ancient ivory. These were no ordinary bones. They had the look of relics. She glanced at the lead sheet that had acted for so long as a makeshift coffin lid. The inscription was in Latin, not properly engraved, scratched in haste. It was too faint to read properly down here, let alone translate, but it was some kind of prayer, or blessing, that much was obvious. A plea for divine protection, but for whom? Against what?

She linked her long fingers under the rounded back of the skull and began to lift.

Tom had gone to join the others, but Davey stayed where he was. He still felt uneasy, kind of queasy, and when Dr Jones touched the skull, he began to feel sick again.

All eyes were focused on her, on what she was doing. So no one noticed when Davey fell forward from the step where he was sitting. He was now on his knees, his eyes tightly shut, his face creased in agony. He clutched at his ears, shaking his head from side to side, trying to escape the penetrating noise. It had started as soon as Dr Jones lifted the skull. It got worse and worse, vibrating through the bones of his own skull like the searing whine of dentist's drill. A high-pitched screaming, less of a sound, more of a sensation, an amplified vibration, until he thought his whole head would split apart.

No one else in the room heard it, but right over the whole site, the guard dogs went crazy: yelping, whining, barking, hitting the wire of their enclosures.

As soon as Dr Jones placed the skull carefully in the box provided by one of her helpers, the terrible screaming stopped, as abruptly as it had started. In Davey's head, other sensations filled the silence, a swift jumble of impressions. Images flashed through his mind, making no sense: bright blood, flecked with dust, pooling on to a packed-earth floor; a jewelled casket in a cage with bars carved from stone; many hands held out, some in pleading, some in prayer.

Then came the sound of monks chanting, many voices shouting, the clash of steel on stone. The faint smell of incense mixed with smoke caught at the back of his throat. Monks moved in solemn procession, carrying a precious burden. Finally darkness filled his head like trickling sand and Davey fell, face down, on to the ground.

# 5

Davey came round to see a ring of faces staring down at him. Mari Jones was kneeling next to him. Her pale face swam into focus. He could feel her cool fingers on his throat, feeling for his pulse. Her brow was creased with concern, her dark green eyes staring into his.

'Are you all right?' she asked when she could see that he was coming round.

'I think so.' His own voice sounded funny, far away and husky. 'I must have fainted, I guess.'

'Yes,' she smiled, her thin angular features softening a little now that he had come round. 'Let's get you up.' She helped him into a sitting position. 'Head forward, down between your knees. Deep breaths. That's it.' She rested her hand lightly on his shoulder. 'Do you still feel dizzy?'

Davey shook his head. He just felt silly. Fainting was such a girlie thing to do.

'Don't feel ashamed,' she said, almost as though she was reading his mind. 'You shouldn't downplay the effect of a fall like that.' She bit her lip. 'We should have taken you home straight away, or to the hospital, to check you were OK. It's my fault. I should have insisted. Once I'm on site and things begin to happen, I suffer from tunnel vision. I'm really sorry . . .'

'No, don't blame yourself. I wanted to stay.' Davey looked up at her. 'I'll be OK, honestly. I'll be fine.'

He had to go on pretending that it was the fall that had caused him to faint. He couldn't possibly tell her what was really wrong with him. He was at a loss to explain it, even to himself. He had always known that he was more sensitive than other people, subject to feelings about things, premonitions, in a way that others were not. It ran in the family – his grandmother could sense things, too. Also, he was a chime child, born as the clock struck midnight, privileged to see ghosts and fairies. Miss Malkin had said so, and she should know. He had first encountered her last midsummer in her true form as the Lady, the Old Grey Man's daughter. Neither human nor ghost, she was something else. He'd had other strange experiences since then, some involving her, some involving others. Maybe these things had sharpened his psychic senses. Now perhaps this bang on the head had acted as an agent, tuning them in, bringing them into focus. That must be it, he thought, because this was new. The intensity of the screaming, followed by the drifting silence of the vision. He had never experienced anything like that before.

'Is there anything else? Something you'd like to talk about?'

Davey looked up, surprised. The whole time he'd been thinking, Dr Jones had been standing there, noting the quicksilver changes flitting over his face, her own expression a mix of curiosity, sympathy and understanding. She was far from stupid; she knew he was hiding something. Davey did not want to lie to her, but she was an archaeologist, piecing the past together through physical evidence, not exactly given to flights of fantasy. He could not tell her about what he had seen, or heard. She would dismiss the screaming skull as hysterical nonsense. She might think he was just telling stories, or even worse, making it all up to get her attention.

Davey's eyes flickered away from her shrewd searching gaze and he responded to her question with a quick shake of the head.

'Whatever.' She smiled down at him, ruffling his hair. 'You take care. We'd better get you home now,' she added. 'I'd take you myself, but I've got to finish up here. Maybe Richard . . .'

Mr Watson promptly volunteered to drive the children home, much to Kate's delight. She got to sit in the front right next to him. She felt her worries for Davey retreat now they were going home and sat back in the soft leather seat, listening to the music playing low on his in-car stereo. Davey sat in the back between Tom and Elinor. Every now and then Mr Watson asked how Davey was feeling. Kate checked her brother in the mirror. He didn't look too bad now.

'Can we come again tomorrow?' she asked as they approached the turn-off for Wesson Heath. 'To the dig, I mean?'

'I don't know . . . It depends . . .' Mr Watson turned on his windscreen wipers and squinted through the rain.

'On what?' Kate asked. He'd better not say because of Davey, she thought, and then felt guilty and selfish. 'We won't be a nuisance. We'll be very careful.'

His face was serious. 'After what happened to Davey, we'd have to see about letting you back. Your mum might have other ideas, for a start, but it's not just that.' His expression relaxed. 'It's the weather.' He adjusted the wipers, the rain was coming down hard now. 'If it's wet, we can't dig.'

'Oh.' Kate found it hard to hide her disappointment. 'Tell you what . . .' Richard Watson thought for a moment. He liked Kate. She was one of his brightest students and one of the few to take a serious interest in the subject. He liked to encourage kids her age, you never knew where it might lead. Her cousins seemed keen enough, and Mari appeared to have taken a shine to her brother. 'We'll ask your mum. See what she says. Then if the weather's fine, and she OKs it, you can come to the dig.' He grinned at Davey in the rear-view mirror. 'I'm sure Mari can find you some surface work to do, scrubbing pottery or something, keep you out of mischief.'

'What if it's not?' Kate stared at the rain on the windscreen. 'Fine, I mean.'

'If it's raining you can come to the museum. Take a look at the behind-the-scenes work. That's just as important, you know, as digging stuff out of the ground. That's if you're interested—'

'Oh, we're interested,' Kate replied, without consulting the others. 'What time?'

'About two, if that suits you.' He looked into the rear-view mirror addressing the back of the car. They all nodded. 'Fine. Just report to the front desk and ask for Mari – Dr Jones.'

'Will you be there?' Kate asked, suddenly shy.

'Wouldn't miss it for the world. For me it's the most important and interesting part of the work. We might even be able to find out who those bones belonged to.'

'Who do you think they belonged to?' Tom asked from the back of the car.

'Well, don't quote me on it, but I think they are the relics of St Wulfric.'

'The one the pilgrims came to see?'

'Yes.'

'Why do you think that?'

'First off, there's not a whole skeleton. And you saw the state the bones were in. They had been specially pre-served.'

'This St Wulfric. What was so special about him?'

'Well, as Mari probably told you, he founded the cathedral in the seventh century. To be honest, he's a bit of a mystery figure. Some doubt his existence alto-gether. There are many stories about him, mostly myth and legend. Very little historical evidence. That's why this find could be of some importance. It's said that he had a dream to build a church on a hill looking over a bend in the river. This whole area was covered in forest back then and he was guided to this place by a bird, or so the story goes, but the head of his order overruled him and said the building should be built on the opposite bank. Every morning, however, the builders found that the stones had been moved back by miraculous means. Of course, there are other reasons for that. Some say that the hill was—'

'A fairy knowe,' Kate said, almost without thinking.

'Yes.' Richard Watson turned to his pupil in surprise. 'How did you know that?'

'Did it at school last year,' Kate said quickly. She could feel herself blushing.

'Well, you're right. Some think early Christian churches were built on pagan sites and then dedicated to heavyweight saints like John the Baptist. His holy day is Midsummer Day, specially chosen, some say, to show the fairies who's boss.' He laughed, but his passengers failed to join in. 'That could be the meaning of the *Agnus Dei*,' he added, suddenly thoughtful. 'Anyway, as I say, building your church on a pagan site was a way of keeping in with the local populace. Not that it did Bishop Wulfric much good.'

'How do you mean?'

'He was attacked at Mass. He was hacked to pieces in his own church. His brains were dashed out in front of his own altar.'

'Ugh! That's horrible!' Elinor exclaimed from the back. 'What do you think, Davey?'

She dug her cousin in the ribs, but he didn't say anything. Maybe he wasn't feeling well again. He'd been quiet all the way back and he'd just gone a distinctly funny colour.

'Who did it?' Tom asked.

'Some say Viking raiders. Others pagan tribesmen under the direction of their own priesthood. Nobody really knows. His remains were gathered together and began to perform miracles almost at once. A shrine arose here very quickly. In its heyday, it would have received thousands of pilgrims a month.'

'What happened to it?'

'The shrine was broken into at the Reformation and the bones removed, whether for destruction, or safe-keeping, nobody knows.'

'This shrine,' Davey asked shakily. 'What did it look like?'

'It's not there now, of course, but I can hazard a guess. I've seen others both here and on the continent. The bones themselves would have been kept in some kind of casket, perhaps of ivory, or precious metal studded with jewels. This would have been placed inside an elaborate shrine carved from stone.'

Davey did not ask any more and he was glad when Kate's teacher stopped the car in front of their house. He left the car in a daze, trying to take in what Mr Watson

had said. He remembered that, after the terrible screaming, just before he fainted, all these images had flashed up
in his head, like a film that made no sense, from the
murder of the saint to the hiding of the relics. The images
had shown him exactly what Richard Watson had just
described. He had seen it all.

138

# 6

Alison Williams, Davey's mum, was very grateful to Mr Watson for taking care of her son. She did not blame anyone at all, she knew that Davey was more than capable of getting into scrapes all by himself, he did not need help from anyone else. Nevertheless, she did feel a visit to the hospital was a good idea, so Davey was whisked off to Casualty and then made to go to bed early.

She watched him like a hawk all the next morning before deciding that there was no harm done. She had doubts about him going back to the dig, but it was raining anyway, so she needn't have worried. The sky was a uniform grey and the rain was thin and fine, the kind that can drizzle all day. Kate and the others were disappointed, but Davey was only too glad. They would get to see what went on behind the scenes in the museum and right now that felt safer to him than poking about in the darker corners of the Old Town.

The City Museum was on Fore Street, up on the right, past the Town Hall and the new Law Courts. It was an imposing structure, square and massive. It had once been the old Court House, home to the regional Assizes. Its outer aspect was still rather grim and forbidding. The windows were few and small, set wide apart in the grey-flecked granite and the figure of Justice still stood blindfold in a niche above the entrance.

Kate pushed the big revolving doors that led into a large, echoing, marble-floored foyer. They had all been here before on rainy day visits like everybody else; but that had been just to look round, now they were here on other business. A big circular information desk stood on its own in the middle of the floor.

Davey, Tom and Elinor hung back, leaving Kate to go first. She was the eldest. It was her job to approach the scary-looking woman on the other side of the wide polished counter. They kept a safe distance, flicking through the leaflets featuring city attractions and forthcoming events.

'Er, excuse me . . .'

'Yes, how may I help you?' The woman wore a name badge on the lapel of her bottle-green suit. *Mrs Marilyn Marchmont, City Leisure and Tourism.*

'We – we've come to see—'

'You'll find guides and activity packs on that pile there,' the woman said quickly, not waiting for Kate to finish her sentence. She turned her attention back to the roster in front of her. She clearly considered herself too important to listen to enquiries from children.

'No,' Kate started again. 'We're not here to look round. We've come to visit . . .'

'The sheets are free, Official Guides £3.50, Children's Fun Packs £1.'

'No.' Kate shook her head. 'We've come to see—'

'Wait a minute, dear. Ah, Dr Monckton . . .'

Kate rolled her eyes at the others. This was hopeless. The woman was putting her on hold to simper at a tall, thin man behind her who was wearing a long black overcoat, almost to the floor. He smiled down at Kate, his eyes crinkling with understanding. A mane of grey hair grew from a point on his forehead, falling on to his shoulders. At first glance, this made him look old, but the face underneath the widow's peak was young. His skin was dark, swarthy, his jaw brushed with five o'clock shadow. He had an inquisitive, questioning expression and a mischievous, almost impish grin, accentuated by high cheekbones and a pointed chin. Thick black eye-brows almost met over dark eyes set deep in his head. His gaze flicked from Kate to the other children, finally focusing on Davey. The boy shifted uncomfortably, his own eyes dropping away from the piercing stare. He had never seen this man before but he had a strange feeling that Dr Monckton knew who they were.

'It's all right, Mrs M, I can wait.' He spoke with a slight Scottish accent; his voice was deep and soft. 'See what this young lady wants first, eh?'

The woman returned his smile and turned back to Kate with barely hidden impatience.

'Well, what is it that you want?'

'We've come to see Dr Jones,' Kate announced crisply. 'She's expecting us.'

'We-ell.' The woman surveyed them suspiciously, shaking her head. Her expression said that children were not to be trusted. 'There's no message on the desk—'

'But she said!' Kate snapped, unable to hide her impatience. 'She's expecting us!'

'What does the old bat think we're going to do?' Tom asked, loud enough for the woman to hear. 'Make off with a load of priceless artefacts?'

Old bat. That did it. Colour washed the woman's powder-caked cheeks and her thin coral-lipsticked mouth disappeared altogether. Her eyes flickered to the uniformed guard standing over in the corner. Kate shot Tom a thanks-a-lot look. They would probably all be thrown out now.

'Why don't *I* take them up?' the man said suddenly. 'If Mari's expecting them, I'll take responsibility.'

'Very well, Dr Monckton,' the woman's tone was icy. '*If* you're sure.'

'No problem.' He signed them in. 'Right, kids, this way.'

Dr Monckton took out a big bunch of keys and used a thin blue plastic security key to unlock the door marked: *Private. Museum Staff Only.* Davey was excited. He had never been through a *Private* door before.

'Are you the kids that helped find those bones yesterday?' Dr Monckton asked as they walked along the corridor.

'Yes, that's right,' Kate replied. 'How do you know?'

'I was helping Mari with the lead tablet they found on top of them, translating the inscription.'

'Oh, yes. What did it say?'

'Turned out to be the Lord's Prayer. The one you probably say in school assembly. Simple but effective. Still the strongest protection against evil. Oldie but a goodie, eh?' he added with a grin. 'You'll find Dr Jones in there.'

He paused by an open door, pointing into a long room with one central table surrounded by a number of work stations armed with computer terminals. The table was covered in a mixture of what looked like lab apparatus: microscopes and instruments, as well as stacks of papers and trays of artefacts. All around, floor to ceiling, stood shelves, holding books, files and boxes.

'I'll leave you here, then . . .'

'What do you do?' Kate asked just as he was going.

'Oh, I'm an archivist. I work with old books and papers.' He laughed. 'There's more ways of digging through the past than freezing your behind off in a muddy field.'

'Do you work in there with Mari?' Davey nodded towards the room in front of them.

'No.' He shook his mane of grey hair. 'I've got my own office further down the corridor.'

'Can we come and see what you do?'

He shook his head again. 'Not just at the minute, Davey. I've got a lot of work on.' He was still smiling as he looked down at them, and his tone remained pleasant and affable, but just for a second his bright, dark eyes seemed to film, as if a screen had come down over them. 'I've got a lot to do and I'd better be getting back to it. Maybe some other time.'

He turned and went on his way down the corridor. Davey watched him go, puzzled by his parting words. They had not introduced themselves properly. Mari Jones might have told him who they were, but she was unlikely to refer to them individually, so how did he know Davey's name? Something told him that there was more to Dr Monckton than met the eye.

Dr Jones was bent over a computer, feeding in data.

'Hello, how did you get in?' she asked as they came in.

'Dr Monckton brought us up,' Kate explained.

'Oh.' The archaeologist nodded. 'I see. He's like a dog with two tails at the moment. Very excited.'

'About this?' Kate looked round.

'No.' Mari Jones shook her head. 'Although he is taking a keen interest. He's got his own project. He's on secondment, kind of on loan if you like,' she explained to their puzzled looks. 'Lent to us by his university. He's an expert archivist and we need his help. Some workmen were renovating one of the houses in the Old Town when they found a room hidden behind some panelling. There was practically a whole library in there, and a treasure trove of documents. Nothing later than seventeenth century, and some of the books are much, much older.

It's a very exciting find. Dr Monckton is going through them at the moment, cataloguing and classifying. It's very much his project.' She laughed. 'He won't let anyone else even take a look. Now,' she stood up, 'would you like to see what we're all up to?'

She took them round then, introducing them to the rest of the team, showing them the different sorts of work being carried out.

'What can we do?' Kate asked. 'We don't want to be in the way.' She looked around at the others. 'We want to do something useful.'

'You can help *me* if you like.' Richard Watson, her History teacher, smiled up from where he was sorting and attempting to match bits of pottery.

'OK.' Kate sat down next to him, she didn't need a second invitation.

'That won't take four of us,' Davey pointed out.

'Anyone good at drawing?'

Elinor nodded.

'You can help Jackie, then.' Mari Jones pointed to a young woman sitting at the end of the table with paper and pencil in front of her. 'She's sketching some of the finds.'

Tom had already drifted off. He was nuts about science at the moment and had been attracted by a pretty heavy duty microscope and an interesting array of equipment and chemicals. He was deep in conversation with a young man with a ponytail who was telling him about the conservation of organic materials. Which just left Davey with nothing to do.

'You can come and help me, if you like,' Mari Jones smiled down at him. 'I'm creating a database, feeding in what we know so far about your bones.'

'They aren't *my* bones,' Davey laughed.

'If you hadn't done your disappearing act we might never have found them. How are you feeling, by the way?' Her face changed to concern. 'All right now?'

'Yes, sure.' Davey smiled. 'I'm fine, thank you.'

Mari looked him over. He certainly looked much better. His pleasant, blunt-featured face had a good colour now. Last night his dark eyes had been cloudy and dull, now they were clear, full of life and interest. She was glad. She felt bad enough about any accident happening when she was in charge of a dig, let alone to a child, and she liked this boy. He looked like any of the kids you could see every day, skateboarding on the museum steps or roller-blading across Market Square — stocky, slightly below average height, with a child's rounded compact build. He no doubt got teased about that, but he was the kind who would probably shoot up to six foot in no time once adolescence kicked in. An ordinary kid, but there was something about him; she sensed a depth, a sensitivity that was hard to define.

'What do you want me to do, Dr Jones?' Davey asked, blushing slightly under her shrewd scrutiny.

'Hmm? Oh.' She turned back to her computer, spreading her long slim fingers over the keyboard. 'You read the figures out and I'll enter them. It's tedious work, but eventually it will pay dividends. And call me Mari,' she smiled. 'Dr Jones is way too formal.'

Davey nodded. He'd try, though it didn't seem natural.

'What are they for?' he asked, pointing to the list of figures.

'I'm creating a database for the bones. Putting in all the measurements. The computer can then collate them and come up with a three-dimensional model of what he would have looked like. Clever, eh?'

Davey had to agree. 'How do you know it's a *he*?'

'We have part of the pelvis. You can tell from that.'

'What else have you found out?'

'We know that the wrapping was linen. We know that he was not buried where we found his bones – they were disarticulated – taken apart from each other – and the skeleton is incomplete. We have sent off a sample of the linen and the bone for carbon dating. The results will take a while to come back, but what we hope . . . what we are hoping to find is . . .' She hesitated. She wanted it so much she could hardly say it.

'That the linen is much more recent than the skeleton?'

'Yes,' she smiled. The boy was bright, too. 'Exactly.'

'Because that might mean that the bones belong to someone special, like St Wulfric?'

'Yes,' her smile widened, 'Richard must have been explaining his relic theory to you.'

Davey nodded. His eyes strayed to the screen saver. 'Do you think it could be true?'

'Yes, Davey, I do.' Her eyes shone and her hands clasped and reclasped themselves in nervous excitement.

'In that case . . .' Davey faltered. His eyes darted to the table where the bones lay and back again, doubt and fear clouding his face. 'Don't you think that you should keep them somewhere safe?'

'Safe?' She looked at him curiously. 'What do you mean?'

'I mean in a special place. Like in a church. In the cathedral, for instance.'

Her forehead wrinkled. What a strange thing to say. 'They will be quite safe here, Davey. Don't you worry.'

Dr Jones kept Davey busy, but eventually the torrent of statistics slackened off. She suggested a break and gave him some money to get her a tea and whatever he wanted from the drinks machine down the hall.

On his way, Davey glanced through the glass doors of the offices on either side of the corridor. They were little more than cubby holes, and most were deserted. When he came to the door marked *Dr Monckton* he slowed down. Davey thought of asking if the man wanted a drink, seeing that he was going to get some, but Monckton was hard at work, bent over a desk stacked high with leather-bound books and stiff bundles of papers. Davey hesitated, not wanting to disturb him, but just at that moment, Dr

Monckton looked up, nervous, startled, as if suddenly aware that he was being watched.

'Can I help you?' he asked from behind his desk.

'No . . . well, yes.' Davey stood in the doorway, wondering whether to go in. The doctor didn't seem very welcoming. 'I was just going to ask you . . .'

Davey's voice trailed away. He had noticed something familiar. In the corner of the room stood a blackthorn staff. It was bigger than a walking stick, fashioned from a single length of thorn wood that had grown twisted, warped away from the true. It was tipped with silver. The handle was silver, too; the strange devices carved upon it worn to faint tracings by much use. Davey felt cold fingers walking over him. He had seen this somewhere before. He was sure.

He stepped forward, wanting a closer look.

'Don't touch!' Dr Monckton shouted, already half out of his seat.

Davey recoiled, the words and the tone jerking him back.

'Sorry, but it has been treated with wood preservative. We wouldn't want to poison you, would we?' Monckton laughed, trying to make a joke out of his unexpected sharpness.

'No,' Davey mumbled.

'Interesting piece, although of no great value,' he added, dismissively. 'More of a curio, really. Not fine enough for exhibition. That's why I keep it in here with me.'

'Where did you get it from?'

'It was found in the city, along with some books and papers and such. Now, how can I help?'

'Oh.' Davey turned to him. 'I just wondered if you wanted a drink.'

'That's very kind.' He looked up at Davey, but he still seemed tense and his smile did not quite reach his eyes. 'Very kind thought, indeed, but I'm off out to the library in a short while. I won't be back for some time.'

'OK.' Davey shrugged. 'Just thought I'd ask.'

'As I say, very kind. Now if you'll excuse me . . .'

He gathered the papers that he had been studying, covering them with a folder, but not before Davey noticed that some of the documents were marked with the same signs to be seen on the silver-headed staff. Davey got the drinks and returned to the archaeologists' room, but their work no longer held his interest as it had done previously. His mind kept going back to where he had seen that staff before. In the house of Judge Andrews.

Known as 'Hanging Andrews' or 'The Executioner', the Judge had been notorious in his own time and after. He had presided over the Assizes, sending hundreds to their deaths, many on an instrument of his own devising, a kind of guillotine, nicknamed 'The Maiden'. Eventually his own crimes had caught up with the Judge. He was tried for witchcraft himself; found guilty in his own court before taking his turn on the gallows. All this was common knowledge, one of the city's more colourful

150

historical corners. It was the stuff of popular story and myth, as told by Louise, the guide on the Haunts Ghost Tour. The Judge's house was one of the regular stops on her tour. That was when Davey had first heard of him, but he also knew things that Louise did not.

The Judge might be dead in the conventional sense, but his evil lived on, and so did his spirit. In the city of ghosts that existed parallel to their own, he was an object of terror and dread, a force to be reckoned with. Davey knew this because he had seen him. A tall man dressed all in black, with a white curling wig and a wide-brimmed hat, and eyes . . . Davey shivered at the thought of them looking at him. Eyes that never blinked, hardly recognisable as human, eyes as pitiless as some great bird of prey.

Davey had stood before him, in his room, waiting for judgement to be given on himself and his two ghost friends, Elizabeth and Polly. The Judge had leaned over a table that held a huge leather-bound book, the *Book of Possibilities*, in which is written *What Was, What Is, and What Is To Be*. He had read from there, fixing Davey with his cold black stare, and all the time, next to him, leaning against the table, had been his twisted blackthorn staff with its polished silver top.

Davey had no idea what Dr Monckton's involvement with the Judge could be, but when the man had looked up from his papers there was a burning, feverish look in his eyes. It was as if something was poisoning him from the inside, and Davey had a shrewd idea that it wasn't wood preservative.

Davey wandered around among the archaeologists, restless, distracted, trying to make up his mind. When he saw the doctor's long figure striding down the corridor, staff in hand, he knew what he must do.

'I have to leave,' he said to Kate.

'What *now*? But—'

'Yes. Now.' Davey already had his coat on. 'You don't have to come with me.'

Kate looked at him. She knew by his expression that arguing would be pointless. In this kind of mood, he would go anyway, with or without company.

'Hang on, I'll get the others.' She grabbed her coat off the back of the chair. If he went on his own, they might never see him again.

'What's all this about?' Kate asked when they got outside.

'What's happening, Davey?' Elinor wanted to know, annoyed at having to abandon her drawing.

'Yeah, Davey, mate. I was getting on great,' Tom complained as he put on his coat. 'What's going on?'

'I'll explain later.' Davey was already heading for the stairs. 'Come on! We've got to hurry!'

# 7

They were downstairs in time to see Dr Monckton turn smartly to the left, away from the library which was further up Fore Street. He cut down Fetter Lane, a narrow alleyway running along the side of the museum.

'We've been here before. On the ghost walk . . .' Kate looked around, recognised the little studded door set into the wall.

'Ssh, Kate!' Davey whispered fiercely. 'He'll hear you!'

'Davey.' She held on to her brother's arm. 'Would you mind telling me why we are following Dr Monckton?

'I think Monckton's in touch with the Judge.'

'What Judge?'

'Judge Andrews. He's got the Judge's staff, or one just like it. I saw it in his room.' He kept his eyes on Monckton's retreating figure. 'It'll take too long to explain now, but I've got a feeling about him. You'll just have to trust me . . .'

Kate looked at Tom and Elinor who both nodded. Their identical green stare showed that they were prepared to do just that.

'Quick, then.' Tom pointed to go forward. 'Let's get moving before we lose him.'

They advanced cautiously, keeping into the sides of the

building, in case Monckton noticed them, but the man looked neither left nor right. He strode purposefully on, passing under a stone archway and on into the heart of the Old Town.

Davey thought that he might be heading for the Judge's house, but he walked straight through Fiddler's Court without even a glance at the tall grey town house where the Judge had once lived. He went straight on, not lingering to look in any shops, keeping the same head-down purposeful stride, as if he was going somewhere specific, and had to get there in a hurry.

He was not hard to follow. Tourists and visitors, here for Easter, filled the narrow streets, slowing Monckton down. His tall figure and distinctive mane of grey hair made him easy to spot in the milling crowds.

They were doing well, then Monckton suddenly stopped. Maybe he had seen them. Davey dodged into a shop doorway, pulling the others after him. Monckton looked round, his eyes flicking over the place where they were hiding. He did not react, or show that he thought himself followed, but he turned sharp right, leaving the street abruptly to enter a narrow alleyway that ran between two rows of half-timbered houses.

'Which way did he go?'

There was no sign of Monckton in the alleyway, or in the street at the bottom.

'I know where we are.' Tom looked up at the houses on either side. 'We came here on the Haunts Tour. *The*

154

*Seven Dials* is back there, or the Tourist Information Office, or whatever it is now. This is Harrow Lane . . .'

The street was cobbled. The half-timbered buildings on either side had thick wooden doors. This was one of the oldest roads in the city. Now a prime tourist area, the houses had been turned into galleries, craft shops, delis and cafés.

'Perhaps he's nipped into one of them,' Kate suggested.

Davey thought for a moment and then dismissed the possibility. You don't stride halfway across the city and then stop to browse in gift shops.

'No.' He shook his head. 'He was going somewhere specific.'

'Keeper's Stairs!' Tom exclaimed. 'It's just down there. We went with Haunts Tours. There's a door set into the wall that lets you into the underground bit. Don't you remember?'

There was no sign of Monckton on the steps, but he could have gone to the street at the bottom. Tom and Davey ran down quickly, taking the steps two at a time. Kate and Ellie stayed at the top, keeping watch.

Tom looked up and down and then turned back with a shake of his head. Each side of the long road was clear. They met in the middle of the steps, stopping in front of the little door in the high stone wall. It was marked now with the Haunts Tours logo. Davey tried the handle. It was locked.

'Try this.' Tom took a plastic card out of his wallet.

'What's that?'

'Leisure centre season ticket.'

'Oh, right,' Davey looked at him. 'Get us in for free, will it? Except I don't see any swimming pool— '

'You use it to open the door, you prat. Slide it down by the side like this.' He inserted the card between the door jamb and the Yale lock. 'At least, it works in the movies. Wiggle it about a bit and . . .' He bent the plastic this way and that and suddenly the lock snicked back. 'We're in!'

Davey grinned. 'Tom, you're a genius!'

They pushed the door cautiously, letting themselves in to the cold narrow passage. Little electric lights came on automatically high on the rough stone walls. They were back in the underground city. They paused, looking round. They had not been here since midsummer; but their experience then had imprinted this place, sight, smell, everything, on their memories forever.

# 8

The subterranean street they were standing in had once been above ground, open to the light and air. For a moment, Davey thought he heard the distant voice of Louise, the Haunts Tours guide, welcoming them again to the terror and mystery of the hidden city.

This place, Cairncross Close, had been sealed off during an outbreak of the plague, all the inhabitants had been bricked up inside and left to die. No one would live there after that, and eventually the whole neighbourhood had been covered over. The houses were still here, under the modern surface of the city. So were the ghosts.

There were none in evidence now, as far as he could tell, but Davey moved forward cautiously, checking the chambers left and right. Then he stopped, motioning the others back against the wall. They were outside a room they had visited before. The Room of Ceremonies was different from the others. Used by a local occult group for their rituals, it was octagonal in shape and the centre of the floor was marked out with a large circle and a five-pointed star. A large ornate gold-framed mirror stood against the far wall.

The iron gate that shut the room off from the underground street was slightly ajar. Davey peered over it warily.

'Is he there?' Tom whispered.

Davey shook his head. The purple-swathed, black-painted room was empty. The iron gate swung back noiselessly, as if it had recently been oiled. They stepped in cautiously. The room smelt of incense. The scent was strong, the musky spiciness overpowering. A fresh incense stick still smouldered in its holder and a wisp of smoke curled up from the stubby wick of one of the huge candles set on either side of the five-pointed star. Whoever had been in here had only recently left, and not by the door, or the children would have seen them. Davey glanced towards the mirror. The surface was misted as it had been before. Far inside, in its deepest recess, something was moving. There was another way out of here . . .

'Wait!' Kate caught his wrist. 'You have to tell us more before we get any further in. How do you know Monckton's in touch with the Judge?'

'He's got the Judge's staff, like I told you. I saw it in his room and he's got it with him now. Dr Jones said Monckton had been working on a secret archive that had been hidden in a house somewhere in the Old Town,' Davey went on. 'She didn't say where exactly, but you don't need to be a genius to work it out.'

'And you think he knows about the mirror? You think he might have . . .'

Kate stared into the misted blackness. This was no ordinary looking-glass, it acted as a portal between two worlds. She knew. She had been through it.

'Used it?' Davey finished her sentence for her. 'What do you think? If we could do it, why couldn't he?'

Kate nodded slowly. It made sense. She had never thought about it before, but there was no reason why the mirror should be exclusive to them. There was no reason why others should not go through . . .

As she watched, something took shape on its misty surface. A tall, black-coated figure. She started away in terror. Monckton was coming back! But instead of getting nearer, his image seemed to be receding. How could that be? Unless, unless . . .

Kate felt fear pour down inside her, chilling her blood to ice. There were two mirrors, fixed at an angle to reflect each other. She turned just in time to see Monckton looming up in the facing glass. A great mane of grey hair swept back from a high forehead; black eyebrows drawn down over eyes staring and intent, the mouth stretched wide in a wolfish curving grin. He was in both mirrors at once! The silver tip of his stick poked through into the room.

Tom and Elinor dived behind a big oak chest by the door. Kate pulled Davey back behind a swathe of purple draping. They all stayed very still, hardly breathing, as the man passed from one mirror into the other. The surface rippled, like mercury, then the figure was enveloped, disappearing into the swirling depths.

'How did he do that?' Without even thinking, Davey leapt to go after him.

159

'Davey! No!'

Kate held on to his coat. As he surged forward, she did not let go. Davey lunged towards the undulating surface, diving into his own reflection, arms outstretched. There was no crash, no sound of breaking, just a bending warp as he took Kate with him and they both plunged straight through the glass.

# 9

They were standing on Keeper's Stairs a step or two above the Haunts Tours entrance, except the door wasn't there any more.

It was like before, at midsummer. The same empty, dusty, deserted atmosphere. The same silence. The same strange yellow-grey half-light, not really day, not really night. The world they were in was similar to the one they had left, but subtly different, and they had no idea how to get out of it, how to get back.

'What are we going to do?' Kate asked her brother.

'Follow him,' Davey replied, already mounting the steps.

'What about Tom and Elinor?'

'What about them? They can look after themselves.' He turned to his sister, reading her thoughts. 'We'll think about getting out after. We're here now. We might as well take advantage of it.'

They approached the top of Keeper's Stairs with caution. Last time, danger had been waiting at the top of the steps. Davey had only just escaped the clutches of the Recent Dead, helped by the mute boy Govan. Now there was no one about at all. No sign of friend or enemy in a Harrow Lane that was oddly changed. They dodged round a corner, keeping close into the wall. Up ahead the black-coated figure of Monckton strode away from them.

'It's him!' Davey leaned out, risking a better look. 'Quick. We've got to get after him!'

They followed him as best they could, trying to keep out of sight, trying to be inconspicious. Being in Ghost City brought more dangers than mere discovery by their quarry. The deeper they went in, the more the dangers multiplied.

They passed the inn of *The Seven Dials*. Davey looked in the dusty diamond-paned windows, hoping to see Jack Cade and his ghost crew inside; but there was no sign of the highwayman, or his companions, Polly, Govan and Elizabeth. The door was locked and the place seemed deserted. Jack and his crew had helped them in the past, Davey had been counting on them doing the same again. But their ghost friends were not around; they would have to go on alone.

'Remember what Jack said,' Davey whispered to Kate, trying to reassure himself as well as her. 'In this world, they are real and *we* are the ghosts. That means even if we do meet some, they probably won't be able to see us.'

'I certainly hope you're right,' Kate whispered back.

They were stuck in Ghost City, isolated, alone, without friends and with no way out. They were following a man who was probably leading them straight to an enemy of the most dangerous kind . . . Kate passed a hand over her eyes. It did not bear thinking about.

When they slipped out of Butcher's Row and into Quarry Street, Davey was sure that they were heading for the Judge's house. This was the way he and Elinor had come with Polly on Midsummer's Eve.

He did not want to get too close to the Judge's house, there might be Sentinels about. He stopped, meaning to tell Kate that they could go back now. That's when he heard it: a kind of pattering, coming along behind and then stopping. They were being followed. He motioned Kate forward, finger to his lips, then stopped again. The light feet stopped, too. He did it again, the same thing happened. Every time they stopped, the sound stopped. Every time they moved, it started up; but when they looked behind, there was nothing there. Worse than that, the more they speeded up, the nearer they got to Monckton. He already seemed wary, looking back now and again, his dark face frowning and suspicious, as if he sensed that he was being shadowed. Whatever he might be, he was no ghost. He would spot them in an instant. Their modern clothes – bright-coloured jackets, blue jeans, white trainers – stood out like splashes of paint in this monochrome world, marking them as different. And he would recognise them for sure.

'We're being followed,' he whispered to Kate.

'I know,' she muttered back.

'Ssh.' Davey put a finger to his lips.

The pattering footsteps were coming on again. Davey

and Kate kept as close to the wall as possible, sheltering in the shadow of the heavy wooden beams jutting out from the eaves of the houses. The footsteps were getting nearer and nearer. Davey nodded towards the next opening on to the street as their best means of escape.

Suddenly Davey dodged under an archway, dragging Kate with him. All around, the upper storeys of ancient buildings frowned down on them. They were in a small courtyard. They looked about, frantically searching for another way out, but this was a dead end. It was too late to go back, the footsteps were nearly upon them. They flattened themselves into an L-shaped recess and stood listening, hardly breathing, hoping that their stalker would go straight past.

Davey sighed with relief as the footsteps went on, but then they faltered, coming to a halt. Step by step they came back, pausing at the open archway, hesitating for a moment or two, and then came on as relentlessly as before. Davey and Kate readied themselves. Their only chance was to burst out, hoping for surprise.

Davey went first, cannoning into a creature not much bigger than himself. His opponent was much lighter than him, with a scrawny, bony body. Davey was strong for his age, and solidly built. He was no stranger to the odd playground ruck and now his blood was up, the will to survive blanking out everything else. He shoulder-charged as if he was on the rugby field, and then grabbed the thing by the throat. The skin felt cold, clammy to the touch, as Davey held it against the wall.

'Quick, Kate! Run for it.' Davey shook the creature like so much rag and made to throw it to the floor.

'Davey! Wait!' His sister was by his side now, tearing his hands away. 'Let go for goodness' sake! Look who it is!'

Gradually the red mist cleared from Davey's head. He relaxed his grip, letting out a shuddering sigh. The huge black eyes staring out above his clamping hand, startled and terrified, belonged to Govan.

'Govan! I'm sorry!' Davey felt utterly contrite. He released the ghost boy, putting his arm around him. 'Are you all right?'

Govan gaped like a fish, hands on knees, gasping for breath, then he nodded.

'What are you doing here?'

It was a silly question on two counts. This was his home, he belonged here, and Govan was mute. He could not answer.

He nodded again, managing a weak smile as his physical distress ebbed. Then the boy's face clouded. Different feelings flitted through his expressive eyes. Happiness at seeing old friends again was replaced by worry, anxiety and fear, but whether for himself, or them, they had no way of knowing.

He looked from Davey to Kate and back again and then

he passed a hand over his eyes and mimed playing the violin.

'The Fiddler! The Blind Fiddler!' Davey guessed. 'Did he send you?'

Govan nodded.

'Hear that, Kate?' Davey grinned as hope leapt like a physical pain in his chest. If anyone could get them out of here, it was the Blind Fiddler.

Govan pointed to them and mimed the world around them.

'What are we doing here?' Kate interpreted. 'Good question. We followed a man. Through the mirror, you know?' Govan nodded for her to go on. 'He's tall, grey-haired but not old, wears a black coat. Do you know him?'

Govan nodded again.

'Does he go to see the Judge?'

Govan nodded more vigorously this time.

'That's what we thought.' Davey took over. 'What for? What business does he have there?'

Govan shrugged, arms spread out. Such questions were beyond his power to answer. Then he cocked his head on one side as if listening, he put a finger to his mouth to indicate silence and his eyes widened into great pools of fear. The time for conversation was over. He drew them back, melting into the shadows under the archway. Heavy footsteps were coming their way, the ring of boots on cobbles, a man's stride, accompanied by the swinging rhythmic tap tap of a staff on the ground. A black-coated figure swept by, marching along the street outside. He was not alone, but his companions made no sound. He was followed by ranks and ranks of shadows.

# 10

Alone in the Room of Ceremonies, Tom and Elinor debated what to do. Instinct told them not to follow their cousins through the mirror. There was no guarantee that they would get back and there was no knowing who might be waiting on the other side. Who knew what dangers the ghost world would hold in store? It seemed safer, more sensible, for two to wait in the here and now. But waiting wasn't easy. Should they remain here or go outside?

Tom thought that they should stay, at least for a while, in case Davey and Kate came back this way. Elinor could see the sense in that.

'But do we have to stay in here?' she asked.

The Room of Ceremonies, bathed in its eerie violet light, with its occult paraphernalia and strange signs, had lost none of its creepiness. Worse than that, a real feeling of evil, of malevolence, thickened the atmosphere, oppressing the heart and chilling the spirit.

Tom felt it, too. He wrapped his arms tightly about himself. The temperature was falling. The cold they were feeling now was way beyond natural.

'There's another thing . . .' Elinor said quietly, as if afraid of being overheard.

'What?'

'I've only just thought of it, but—'

'But what?'

'When we went through, you know, the last time—'

'Ye-es.'

'When we were in the ghost city, it seemed like a long while, but when we came back . . .'

'It was like no time had elapsed . . .' Tom finished his sister's sentence for her. His own alarm matched the fear on her face.

'Exactly. The only question is—'

'Who'll be back first . . .'

Tom was suddenly aware of a subtle change in the room. The face of the mirror was darkening. The misty surface seemed to thicken and swirl. A figure appeared deep inside, coming nearer with every stride . . .

'You're right. Let's get out of here.' Tom grabbed his sister and sprinted for the door.

Dr Monckton came out of the mirror and looked around him, alert and furtive. Behind him the mirror was unreflecting, filled with ebony blackness. He moved to the side, as if making way for others behind him. Tom and Elinor dived for a room across the stone corridor and lay huddled on the cold earth floor, as wave after wave of black-clad Sentinels stepped out of the mirror.

'What are we going to do?' Elinor asked in a whispered squeak. 'What if they see us here?'

'Ssh.' Tom put his finger to his lips and risked a look.

The black-hooded figures were flowing forward, forming into a phalanx. They were snuffing and sniffing, scenting for enemies; Monckton was leading them, his bright dark eyes darting this way and that. Suddenly, they all froze and stood, poised and quivering. The hooded heads moved as one, slowly, deliberately. Monckton's beady black eyes followed the line of their seeking. Tom could look no more. He put his arm round his sister, who let out a stifled sob of panic. They were seconds away from discovery.

The twins stayed like that, ears stopped by terror, heads buried in each other's shoulders. All the time footsteps were getting nearer. Sound travelled oddly in the tunnels. Tom could hear voices now, getting louder. One voice in particular filtered into his consciousness. He risked another look. Sentinels don't talk.

Across the stone passage, in the Room of Ceremonies, there was no sign of Monckton, but the walls were lined with blackness deeper than shadows, deeper than the flaking paint that adorned them. The walls were an unreflecting matt, as though covered in a deep layer of soot. Cold emanated from the room as if someone had left the freezer door open, but the mass of Sentinels remained still, unmoving, as the Haunts Tour shuffled past.

Tom grabbed Elinor and they slotted in behind as the

group of tourists came to the end of the afternoon ghost walk.

'I apologise for a shorter tour than usual,' Louise, the guide, was saying. 'We will have to leave via the entrance. Our normal exit is unavailable due to essential maintenance work. This way, please.'

Essential maintenance work! Louise's face twisted in a private ironic grin. The whole place was falling down. Plus it was freezing. She drew her black cloak round her ample frame. It got colder down here every day. She whisked her party past the Room of Ceremonies, frowning to discourage any lingering. She particularly disliked that room. Frequented as it was by who knows what kind of weirdos, stinking the place out with their horrible joss sticks. She wrinkled her nose in disgust. That room was *really* creepy!

She shepherded her flock out on to Keeper's Stairs in double-quick time, counting them through before carefully securing the door. The group stood blinking in the afternoon sunshine, most of them glad to get out. It had not been a happy tour. As they stood about, she checked them again, doing a quick head count. Funny. She seemed to have acquired two more from somewhere. Oh, well, she shrugged, it was better than *losing* two. That had never happened, thank God. Except once, last summer, when that kid had dodged off. Turned out he'd just gone outside but it was a close call. Losing someone underground – that would be a *true* nightmare!

171

The group dispersed and Louise trudged off back to the Market Square and her next stint. She was seriously thinking about packing it in as a Haunts Tour guide. She didn't have to do this. The money was rubbish and she was an actress really – well, a drama student at the moment, but it amounted to the same thing. All that excavating was making the tunnels unsafe. As if that wasn't bad enough, it was getting seriously strange down there. Weird things were happening all the time now. All kinds of folk were seeing things, sensing presences, changes in temperature. And these were ordinary punters, not mediums, or students of psychic phenomenon. At this rate, she'd be seeing things herself. Louise shook her head. If things got any weirder, she would be giving in her notice.

## 11

Davey and Kate stayed hidden in a doorway until Govan came back and signalled that it was safe to go out. They thought at first that he was taking them back to Keeper's Stairs and the Room of Ceremonies, but he turned in under the sign of *The Seven Dials*. Perhaps it had not been deserted, after all.

The Blind Fiddler was sitting in the inn's cobbled courtyard, occupying a bench under the overhanging upper gallery that extended round the whole area. He was leaning against the milky brown plaster and weathered wood of the wall, his long wooden staff next to him. One hand trailed in the ivy that writhed up the stair, winding round the banisters and the gnarled carved newel post, the other rested on his violin. He had his eyes closed, as though enjoying the sun in a world where it never shone. An eyelid flickered at their approach, and his face, weathered and lined with age, softened into a smile. His hand stirred the leaves in greeting.

'Ah, Davey, Kate, how do you fare? I've been waiting. Sit down here. We have much to speak about.'

Davey looked round cautiously.

'Do not fear. You are safe here. Now. What is your interest in this man Monckton?'

The Fiddler listened as Davey told him about meeting Monckton in the museum, and how the papers the man was working on had been found in the Judge's house. And how Monckton was using the Judge's staff, Davey had recognised it, and that was what had convinced him to follow.

'I begin to see.' The Fiddler nodded, his blind eyes rolling in his head. 'This Monckton has been given the Judge's books and papers. Within them he has discovered certain knowledge that enables him to enter here. He has made contact with the Judge, who has agreed to help him.'

'But why?' Davey asked. 'For what?'

The Fiddler rubbed his chin, and thought for a while.

'I do not know what he seeks to gain, but depend upon it, the Judge will offer him everything from great wealth to eternal life. Tell me, what is he like, this Monckton?'

'I don't know really.' Davey shrugged. 'I only met him today. He's, well—'

'Scholarly,' Kate supplied. 'That's how I'd describe him.'

'Ah, he will want knowledge, then. The most dangerous thing of all. Seeking after knowledge of that which is secret, forbidden, has led many to perdition. In his day, the Judge was a great scholar himself. He was very learned, delving deep into life's mysteries, but he chose the left-handed path. He amassed many rare books in the pursuit of his studies, and wrote much himself. Pointing the way

174

for any clever man who chanced upon them and who was inclined to take the same sinister route.' He paused. 'The Judge will want something in exchange . . .'

'Like what?'

'Who knows?' The Fiddler spread his fine long-fingered hands. 'He will want him to obtain some item or perform some task. Something only a living man can do.' He thought for a moment before speaking again. 'The recent excavations have been the source of much disturbance here. They have caused upset to any number of spirits. It is rumoured now that there has been some great discovery, deep under the heart of the city.' He turned his head to the two of them. 'Do you know what it might be?'

'Yes.' Davey looked at him. 'We were there when they found it. They think that it is a relic—'

'A relic?' The Fiddler sat forward. 'Of what? Of whom? Do you know?'

'Well, they have tests to do, and that, but they think it's the remains of St Wulfric.'

'Taken from the cathedral? The great church of St John?'

'Yes. Well, that's what they think, at any rate. It must be pretty important.' Davey dropped his voice to whisper, 'When I first saw it, there was a Sentinel kind of hovering over it.'

'Ah.' The Fiddler leaned on his staff, blind eyes gazing unseeing into the distance. 'Things begin to come clear—'

'How?' Davey shook his head. 'I don't see at all.'

'Never mind.' The Fiddler's smile was enigmatic. 'I should know by tomorrow. Be in the Market Square, three hours after noon, and I will have more to tell you. Now you must go. You have been too long in Ghost City already. Much longer and you will attract attention. The Judge has already acquired one living servant, I do not intend to give him more.' As he stood up, Govan stole back to his side. 'We have to get you back to your own time. And then,' he put his hand on Govan's shoulder and the boy smiled up at his master, 'we have work to do, Govan and I.'

They left *The Seven Dials*, walking out under the creaking inn sign. Davey asked where the others were, Jack and Elizabeth and Polly. But the Fiddler either did not know, or did not feel inclined to say. He remained distracted, deep in thought, as Govan led them into a crooked filth-strewn alley.

About halfway down, set into the wall, was a deep stone basin, fringed with ferns. Water trickled from a mouth carved in a face so old and water-worn that it could have been anything, beast or man. This was the Johnswell, it gave the passage its name, but neither Davey nor Kate had ever seen it. The well had been capped and the waters diverted long before their day.

The Blind Fiddler stopped in front of it, arrested by the cool smell and trickle of water. He stood for a moment, head bowed, then he said, 'This is a holy well dedicated to

St John, who still gives his name to it. Story tells us that St Wulfric stopped here as he journeyed through the forest in search of the place where he was to found his church. He was weary, footsore, thirsty, about to give up. He sat down to rest and then suddenly, out of the forest, a man appeared. He was bearded and rough-clad in skins, of wild and fearsome appearance, and carrying a heavy staff. He asked Wulfric for bread. Wulfric had little, barely enough for himself, but he offered to share gladly, only regretting that he could offer the stranger no water to slake his thirst. The man said no matter, and stuck his staff in the ground. A spring, pure and limpid, gushed up from the place where the staff rested and it has been giving water ever since. Wulfric believed that the stranger was John the Baptist and dedicated his church to him. This is his well. Even as it is now, a very special and holy place. Now, search in your pockets. What do you find there?'

They both delved. Kate came up with a fifty pence piece. Davey had no money, only a marble and a football medal his dad had got with petrol.

'That will do. Now, cast them into the basin as an offering. Ask for St John's blessing and wish to be back in your own time.'

The shadows about them were gathering. They did what he said without question . . .

# 12

Davey and Kate found themselves being jostled by pas-
sers-by, surrounded by street noise, staring at a blank stone
wall. Above a lighter patch in the rough grey surface, a
City Heritage plaque read: *Site of the John's Well. An ancient
holy well, for many centuries the principal water supply to this
area of the city. Destroyed in the nineteenth century after it was
identified as a hazard to public health.*

They appeared so suddenly that a woman bumped into
them.

'Sorry,' she said, automatically, then her face registered
recognition. 'Hello,' she said with a surprised smile.
'Where did you two spring from?'

It was Mari Jones, the archaeologist.

'Oh,' Davey smiled back, 'we were just hanging
around. What are you doing here?'

'I live round here. I've got a flat above the Tourist
Information Office . . .'

Davey looked up sharply, eyes widening.

'*The Seven Dials?*' Kate asked before she could stop
herself.

'Well, yes . . .' Mari pushed her red hair back out of her
eyes. Her brows met in a puzzled frown. 'It was called
that. It was a pub once. A long time ago now. My, you do

know a lot about the city.' She viewed Kate quizzically. 'Regular walking gazetteer. Ever thought of giving tours?'

'Oh, I don't know about that . . .' Kate mumbled, blushing furiously.

'We were looking for our cousins,' Davey said to cover Kate's confusion. 'We kind of got separated. You haven't seen them by any chance?'

'I have, as it happens. They were in the Market Square. I saw them when I came out of the cathedral.'

'Oh?' It was Davey's turn to look quizzical. 'What were you doing in there?'

'We-ll.' The archaeologist suddenly felt awkward. She cleared her throat in a nervous half-laugh and looked down, scuffing the ground with her work boot. 'I took your advice. I don't know why. I was going to do it anyway, show them, I mean. I took the bones, the relics,' she said quickly. 'Left them with the Provost for safe-keeping.'

She looked at them, her green-brown eyes challenging, almost defiant. She had acted purely on impulse, a thing she very rarely did, and her motives had been highly unscientific. Her action had been purely intuitive and in her profession intuition was frowned upon. The idea had come to her so suddenly, so strongly, that she had done it almost without thinking. It had felt so right at the time, but now it left her feeling rather stupid.

Davey's eyes met hers. She was an adult, and he didn't know her very well, but he wanted to say, 'Well done.'

179

She caught his look and glanced away. There was something about him that was *very* unsettling.

'We did a dig here once. When they put that plaque up.' She nodded towards the Johnswell, changing the subject. 'Turned up all kinds of interesting stuff, coins, pins, jewellery, put there almost like oblations, offerings to the gods. Well,' she looked around, 'I'd better get off. I was just going to the deli on Harrow Lane. Richard's coming round tonight for supper. Will I see you tomorrow?'

Davey nodded. 'Just one thing,' he added, putting a hand out as she turned to go. 'Do you know if the bones definitely belong to St Wulfric?'

'Not yet.' She shook her head. 'We haven't got the test results back, but I'd say it's a pretty safe bet. See you tomorrow.'

'If we can.' Kate nudged Davey. He had obviously forgotten that Mum had the next day earmarked for a family outing. 'Depends what our mum says.'

'Whatever. I'll be at the site in the morning and then at the museum all the afternoon. See you.'

'Yes, see you,' Kate and Davey said together.

They found Tom and Elinor sitting on the steps of the Market Cross.

'I thought we'd lost you forever!' Ellie said, laughing now, although when her cousins disappeared through the mirror that had seemed a distinct possibility.

'Well, we're back now. You'll never guess—'

Davey broke off, looking from one face to the other. 'What happened?' Kate asked. 'What's up?'

Tom drew them away from the crowds, to a quiet part of the square where they were less likely to be overheard, and told them about Monckton and the Sentinels.

'There's a whole load of them loose somewhere.' Tom looked round warily as if some might be behind him.

Davey frowned. That was not good news. He did not know what Monckton intended, but he was almost certain that the Judge had sent his evil cohorts into this world to help him steal the relics. The Fiddler might be able to tell them more tomorrow. That's if Mum could be persuaded to come up to the Old Town instead of doing whatever she had planned. Davey decided to worry about that later. He glanced up at the great grey stone front of the cathedral. Carved ranks of saints stood in rows, worn faces staring down, fingers held in blessing, or pointing up to heaven. No evil force would dare to invade such a holy place. The bones were safe for now.

## 13

Getting Mum to pay the Old Town a visit was not as difficult as they had anticipated. She declared it 'a lovely idea', but not before giving Davey one of her quizzical looks. When she had suggested a trip not long after New Year, he had positively refused to go near the place. He could be a strange child at times, she thought, governed by sudden unaccountable whims and quick mood changes. Perhaps it was just a phase and he'd grow out of it. Phase or not, it could get distinctly wearing, like all the fuss he'd made about being in that Christmas pageant thing. Well, he seems happy enough now, she reflected, as she drove them to the city.

She parked in one of the New Town's multi-storeys, putting money into the Pay and Display. Parking in the Old Town was next to impossible at the best of times, never mind now with all this redevelopment work going on. She had not seen that yet and wanted to know what was being planned. It was one of her reasons for the trip. She stopped at the big hoarding just inside Cannongate, studying the proposed changes.

'Where's this dig you've been on about?'

Kate showed the approximate place on the map.

'Can we go and have a look? It would be nice to see

what they are doing. And I'd quite like to see Mr Watson, thank him properly for looking after Davey. Such a charming young man . . .'

Kate caught Elinor's eye and winked. There were always mums queuing up at Richard Watson's table. Mums thought he was 'dishy'.

'And that Dr Jones you were talking about? I'd like to thank her, too—'

'Maybe later, Mum.' Davey linked her arm. 'Let's go to Market Square first.'

He set off briskly, practically dragging his mother up Fore Street towards the cathedral. The Blind Fiddler had said three hours after noon, and it was practically that already. If Mum got talking to Watson, they would be lucky to get away before nightfall.

'Hang on a minute, Davey.' Alison Williams looked down at her son. She knew when she was being hijacked, even if she didn't know why. 'What's so special about the Market Square?'

'They've opened up the outdoor cafés,' Kate said brightly with her sweetest smile. 'We could have a cup of tea in the sunshine.'

'That's the best suggestion I've heard all day,' her mother smiled back. 'I could certainly do with one . . .'

What a brilliant idea. Davey shot his sister a grateful look. He never thought of things like that. Sometimes Kate bordered on genius.

★　　★　　★

One side of Market Square was scattered with tables and chairs from open air cafés, just as Kate said. Mum led them towards *Gino's*, the Italian place on the corner where they usually went. Davey hesitated, looking round for the Blind Fiddler and Govan, who was bound to be with him. He could see no sign of them, even though the cathedral clock said quarter past three.

'Come on, Davey,' his mother called back to him. 'Stop dawdling or we won't get a place.'

A big party of tourists, set free from a guided tour, were descending on the cafés like flocking starlings. They got to *Gino's* just in time.

'We're a bit tucked away here,' Davey complained.

'We were lucky to find a table at all,' his mother commented without looking up from the menu. 'Now, what do you want?'

Ordering and waiting took a long time, but there was still no sign of Govan or the Fiddler. Davey shifted in his seat, restless and impatient, trying to get a better view of the Market Square.

'I don't understand you sometimes, Davey.' His mother looked at him over her tea cup. 'It was your idea to come here and now you won't settle. Stop fidgeting about and eat your ice cream before it melts . . . Oh—' she broke off what she was saying and put her cup down. 'What lovely music! Where is it coming from?' She forgot her irritation and looked round eagerly, trying to locate the source.

The music was soft but oddly penetrating; the tune soaring and sad at the same time. A song of loss and longing played on a violin. The high shrill sweetness of a penny whistle stitched in and out of the melody, embroidering the plaintive air with its own complex pattern of notes.

'I know that tune!' his mother exclaimed. 'This takes me back! It reminds me of when my friend Sheila used to play in an Irish band. This used to be one of my favourites. Oh, what is it? It's on the tip of my tongue! Here, Davey—' She reached in her bag and took out her purse. 'Go over and give them this,' she held out some change, 'and ask for the name of that tune.'

Davey took the coins in his hand and approached the Market Cross. He skirted the Haunts Tours board, which stood in its normal place although the space after *Next Tour* was blank. Underneath someone had scrawled: *Cancelled due to ill health*.

The musicians had attracted quite a crowd. Davey had to fight his way through to the front. Coins and notes filled the battered broad-brimmed hat. Davey threw his money in with the rest. The old man played with his eyes closed, his snow-white hair flowing over his shoulders. He gave a slight nod of acknowledgement and Govan's huge black eyes slanted in a smile. Davey stood quietly, waiting for them to finish.

The Fiddler lowered the violin, nodding and smiling as the money chinked in. He waited for the crowd to drift away before speaking to Davey.

'Meet me in the cathedral, I have much to tell you,' he said, then tucked the violin back under his chin. 'The tune your mother so admires is called *Carrickfergus*. A fine old tune. She has excellent taste. Ask her if she knows this. It is for her.'

The swooping, soaring bow drew out the notes, soft and low, then the whistle took over: pure, clear, bittersweet. Even without words, it was possible to know what the song was about: love lost, never to be regained. Davey couldn't help it, he felt his eyes sting. When he got to the table, his mother was blinking tears away, too.

'He said that the last song was called *Carrickfergus* and that this one's for you.'

'*She Moves Through the Fair*, another of my favourites. How did he know? That boy certainly can play . . .' She sat back, eyes closed, until the last echoing note faded away.

'What do you want to do now?' Alison Williams asked when they were ready to go.

'I thought we might go and look round the cathedral . . .' Davey ventured. They all stared at him, varying degrees of amazement showing on their faces. 'Tom needs to go in for a project he's doing at school. Don't you?'

'Well, er, yes, er—' Tom started and then looked round helplessly. Davey's sharp kick to the ankle had prompted an immediate response but failed to suggest what it might be.

'Church architecture,' Elinor supplied. 'He's supposed to collect postcards and that. As examples.'

'Why didn't you say?' His aunt smiled at him.

'Kind of forgot.' Tom could feel himself blushing.

'Come on, then.' Alison Williams led the way across the square. 'I haven't been in for ages, but we can't stay too long.' She checked her watch. 'I have to be back to pick up Emma. And there's not much time left on the car-park ticket.'

As they entered the great west doors of the Cathedral of St John the Baptist, Davey automatically looked upwards. He was captivated, as he was on each visit, by the breathtaking sense of immense size and space. Delicate fluted columns flew upwards, meeting overhead in elegant archways, dwarfing the people below, caging light and air within the confines of stone.

Across from the entrance, Govan was emptying handfuls of money into the box put out to take donations for the cathedral's upkeep. As Davey came up, he grinned in greeting and nodded towards the left-hand aisle.

Davey found the Blind Fiddler in a quiet little side chapel. He was sitting forward in his seat, deep in prayer or contemplation. He did not move as Davey approached him, only a slight incline of the head showed that he knew when the boy was near.

Davey moved the soft felt hat and sat down next to him.

'Well,' he said. 'Do you have news for me?'

'Yes, Davey. Yes, I do. The bones that you have discovered are indeed those of St Wulfric. They should be here, resting in this place of ancient peace. Here in this very chapel.' He inclined his great white head to a blank recess in the grey wall behind the altar. 'This was his shrine for many centuries, until his bones were taken, their resting place desecrated.' He paused for a moment. 'I have many friends here among the dead and the living and they tell me the bones were brought here last evening.'

'That's right, by Dr Jones. She's the archaeologist.'

'Well, she has removed them. For tests.' He grimaced. 'Whatever that means. Do you know if she plans to return them again?'

'I don't know.' Davey shrugged. 'I could find out, I suppose.'

'Do so.' The blind man gripped his shoulder. 'Tell her, tell her that they *must* rest here.'

'Why? Have you found out what the Judge plans to do with them?'

The Fiddler nodded. 'But it is not him I fear.'

'Who then? Monckton?'

'Not him either. There is another—' The Fiddler stopped again, his hand to his mouth, his face full of troubled apprehension. 'I should have known by the nature of the find. I should have realised.'

'Known what? Realised what?' Davey questioned, unsettled by the Fiddler's expression.

'There is someone else involved.' He settled back, his

188

sightless eyes moving as if scanning some internal scene only he could see. 'There was once a man. He stood tall, well over six feet when he was a boy, little more than your age. He was dark-haired, and pale-skinned; very handsome, with large lustrous eyes set wide in a face that was all planes and hollows. He was very thin; his wrists showed like reeds from his fine linen sleeves. Even as a youth he seemed consumed by something from within. He came from one of the greatest noble families in the land, but he was a younger son, destined for the church. He joined a religious order, becoming plain Brother Robert, but he was ill-suited to the contemplative life. He grew from a haughty, prickly novice boy to a proud and clever man with a restless and subtle mind, ambitious for worldly power. This he gained, both for himself and his House. He became Prior here and gold poured into the coffers. He had the ear of kings and princes and was held in high regard in the councils of this land and beyond. His priory was among the richest in England, but it was also notorious. As Prior Robert's wealth and power grew, there were those who said he played most foully for it . . .'

Davey looked up, enquiringly.

'Through the exercise of black arts,' the Fiddler said in explanation, sensing the boy's question. 'Through traffic with the evil one. Then, at the very height of his power, some great spell went disastrously wrong. Prior Robert overreached himself. He disappeared, along with his disciples. The room where they had gathered was scorched from floor to ceiling, but empty of life. He is the chief of those we call the Sentinels. The others are his followers, condemned to roam between this world and the next, as we all have been.' He fell silent and leaned forward, resting his forehead on hands clasped as if in prayer.

'I still don't understand,' Davey said after a moment or two. He was reluctant to interrupt the old man's contemplation, but time was short. 'What has this to do with the relics?'

'Much as black magicians will desecrate and reverse the very cross of Christ our Lord in their corrupt and evil practices, so the Judge and Prior Robert want to use these most holy relics for a dread, fell and evil purpose, but they cannot take them from your world. They need the help of a living human being, that is where your Dr Monckton comes in. The only place where the relics would be safe is here, in this holy church. Tell me, where will Dr Jones, your archaeologist friend, have taken them?'

'To the museum, I suppose.'

'And Monckton works there?'

Davey nodded.

The Fiddler sighed and passed a hand over his blind eyes. 'The museum suits their purposes well. It was once Judge Andrews' courthouse. He sent many to the gallows from there. It is soaked in his evil. Some say his body was returned after his death and is there still, hidden inside the walls . . .' The old man's voice trailed away and his parchment-pale face grew even paler. His long hand trembled as he groped for Davey's shoulder.

'What is it?' Davey asked in alarm. 'What's the matter?'

'I begin to have an inkling of their intention—'

'What? What is it?'

The Fiddler did not answer directly.

'I must be wrong,' he spoke almost to himself. 'What I fear cannot happen. It is forbidden. Even the Judge and Prior Robert . . .' He turned back to Davey with new urgency. 'You must act now.' His grip tightened on the boy's shoulder. 'You must prevent Monckton from getting his hands on the bones of St Wulfric. The holy relics must not remain in the museum. They must be brought here where they belong, and it must be done before the setting of the sun.'

'But how?' Davey could feel panic building inside him. Monckton was a grown man. How could a boy stop him?

'Appeal to the woman. Dr Jones. There is more to her than at first surmise. She will believe you.'

Davey shook his head, far from convinced. She'd never believe him over Monckton. Despite what the Fiddler said, it was Davey's experience that adults stuck together.

'What about my mum? She'll want us to go home . . .'

'I'm sure you will think of something,' the Fiddler said. A wave of his hand, brushing Davey's objection away as trivial.

'What about,' Davey dropped his head, mumbling the real reason for his reluctance, 'what about the Sentinels?'

191

Davey was afraid of them. He had to admit. He was not surprised that they had their origins in a pack of evil corrupted monks. Their dark forms, cowled and robed, were the very distillation of his earliest terrors. The thought of Prior Robert, the tall, gaunt Chief of them, made his heart clench with fear.

The Blind Fiddler groped for Davey's hand.

'I know I ask much of you,' he said, keeping his voice low. 'But I will muster what help I can. Jack and his crew, perhaps others too. They will come if you need them, never fear.'

Davey felt somewhat reassured. He thought for a moment more.

'All right, then,' he said. 'I'll do what I can.'

'Good boy.' The Fiddler patted him on the shoulder. 'I knew we could rely on you. Goodbye, Davey. And good luck.'

'I'll just square it with Mum.'

'Yes. You do that . . .'

As soon as the boy was gone, the Fiddler's brows drew together in a deep frown. The forces ranged against them were formidable. All the Sentinels had left the city, following their leader into this world. In such numbers, they would present difficulties to Jack and his crew. He closed his eyes, focusing his inner sight on Davey. Normally, he would not have involved a child; but the Judge and Prior Robert had recruited Monckton to their service. Living humans could go to places and do things that a ghost would find impossible. Without some kind of human intervention from the other side, the evil they intended to work would be unstoppable. He leant forward, head on folded fingers, preparing to pray. Young as he was, this boy was the only hope they had.

## 14

'The museum is closing.'

'We know,' Kate pleaded, 'but we have to see Dr Jones. It's very important.'

'I'll see if she's still there.' Derek, the uniformed attendant on duty, was far more sympathetic than the woman who had been on the desk before. He smiled at Kate as he picked up the phone. 'She says to go up. Here—' He took keys from his pocket and let them into the private area of the museum.

'Hello.' Mari Jones was there to meet them at the top of the stairs, her brows drawn together in questioning doubt. 'What on earth are you doing here?'

'We came to see—' Davey started to say, but before he could explain further a sudden sickening pain forced him to stop. He bent double, hands to the side of his head. The screaming was so loud, he thought his ears would bleed and his eardrums explode with the intensity of it.

'Davey?' The archaeologist leaned over him, her surprise at seeing them overtaken by shock and concern at the boy's sudden collapse. 'Are you all right?'

He looked up at her, his waxen face creased in agony.

'The bones,' he managed to say. 'Where are they?'

'With Dr Monckton,' she said, frown lines deepening. 'He asked to look at them. Wait! What's the matter?'

The screaming was becoming less intense, losing its bitter edge. Davey managed to recover enough to stagger past her as far as Monckton's office. He hung in the doorway, looking in. The bones were there, but the skull had gone. So had Dr Monckton.

'He's taken it. We're too late.' He crumpled down in despair and would have fallen if Tom and Kate had not caught him.

Mari Jones looked into Monckton's office. The boy was right. The bones were still in their tin storage box, but there was no sign of the skull. What was going on here? Why had these children suddenly rushed in? Frowning again, she glanced over to Davey. What was the matter with him? Why was he so agitated about the skull? There could be some quite simple explanation as to where Monckton might have taken it.

'Perhaps it's in my office. Perhaps he returned it.'

Dr Jones turned on her heel, striding back down the corridor. She scanned her room: the work stations and table were all cleared away for the night. She could tell at a glance that the skull was not there.

She looked down at the children standing beside her. 'I don't understand. I think you'd better tell me what's happening—'

Before anyone could reply, there was a crash behind her. She whirled round, eyes widening. Explanations would have to wait until later. The galvanised security shutters were slamming down of their own accord, one after another. The shutters were not supposed to descend until everyone had left the building. They covered the doors that led to the public galleries. They covered every way out of here.

'Quick! The lift!'

She led them to a wide square door at the end of the corridor. They could hear the whine of machinery as the lift engaged, but none of the buttons responded. It was as if someone, or something, was sealing them in, isolating them from the outside world . . .

'This way.' She pointed to narrow iron spiralling stairs. 'We'll have to go down to the basement and pray that it is still open.'

The public galleries were shutting for the evening. Derek, the attendant, went round locking doors, turning off the lights, leaving the glass cases and different exhibition areas deep in shadow. This was one of his daily duties, and he normally did not think twice about it. Some of his colleagues disliked being in the galleries by themselves in the quickly gathering dusk, mindful of what the cabinets contained, items and artefacts from a bygone age, and the building's long unhappy history. Some would not go past certain tableaux, swearing they had seen the figures move; others said that they had seen the old Judge himself and heard the cries and groans of those condemned by his cruel Assizes. Derek did not hold truck with any of that. He was not a superstitious man, and did not scare easily.

Nevertheless, this evening found him feeling slightly nervous, unsettled even. His feeling of unease grew as he went deeper through the silent galleries. First he was alerted to a sudden drop in temperature, but put that down to a glitch in the air conditioning. Then he began to hear things: soft kind of skitterings. And see things. Every so often, something, or someone, seemed to move in the very corner of his eye, just at the outer range of his vision. If he turned his head, however quickly, there was nothing there. He was confronted by empty space, except, except . . .

He blinked. The darkness seemed to be gathering. In the corners it was black as night. It should not be this dark. His eyes flicked up to the windows set high in the walls. Outside it was still light. Derek made himself go to the furthest gallery. He glanced quickly through the double doors. In there it was as black as pitch. Something was moving, stirring deep within . . .

He wiped a line of cold sweat from under his cap. His legs were wobbling under him, but he began walking back with all the dignity he could muster. Then he heard a noise: a hissing exhalation, or a deep intake of breath. He took one more look and turned and fled. Behind him, ghosts were gathering. The Sentinels were taking over the museum.

★   ★   ★

197

Dr Jones led the way to the basement, wondering what on earth was going on. Why would Monckton want to remove the skull? And what was happening to the security systems? What were these children doing here? With an effort, she put such questions aside. Her major concern right now was to find a way out of the building.

She stepped from the end of the winding stairs into a wide L-shaped area. In front of her was the loading bay, next to that the emergency exit. Metal shutters covered both of them and Dr Jones did not have the necessary keys. Only certain staff had those, and they had probably all gone home by now. She looked again, only to confirm something that she already knew. All the windows were covered by sturdy steel bars and thick wire grilles. They were effectively trapped inside. The museum was very hot on security, but no way in meant no way out. She reached for a phone on the wall. Derek, the evening duty attendant, was their last hope. If he had gone, too, they would have to stay here all night. At one time there had been a guard on duty twenty-four hours a day, but that was deemed unnecessary now. Yet another saving in the budget.

The phone was dead, just as if the wires had been cut. They had no contact with the outside world. She leaned for a moment, eyes closed, mentally checking her knowledge of the place. There were more phones in this area, but they were in the lower basement. One internal, by the stairs and lift, and one in the maintenance man's office. There could be keys there as well . . .

'Come on.' Mari Jones led the way down the last twists of the spiral stairs to the floor below.

She tried the phone on the wall at the bottom of the stairs. As dead as the other one. There must have been some kind of circuit failure. The lower basement was a large area but it was a packed labyrinth, every inch of space taken up. The air was filled with the thrum and hum of different machinery: boilers, air conditioners, humidifiers and dehumidifiers, all working to control temperature and humidity in the floors above. There were large treatment tanks, filled with chemical solutions, and much of the rest of the space was given over to storage. Only a tiny percentage of the museum's collection was on display at any one time. The rest was kept here, or on the floor above, stored in a complex system of moveable shelving. There was little room to move around and it was easy to get lost if you did not know your way about.

The maintenance man's office was tucked in a corner, right over on the other side.

'You stay here,' she said, preparing to thread her way over there. 'And don't touch anything.' She nodded towards the computerised control panels winking with little green lights. 'Some of the chemicals stored down here are dangerous – and keep away from that.' She indicated the ranks of moveable shelving operated by large three-spoked wheels set in the sides of them. 'Roller racking can be a death trap.'

They nodded obediently, promising to stay put. She set

199

off on her mission, too preoccupied to notice the whirr and hum of the lift in motion join the other sounds. It stopped, followed by the muffled bang and clang of a metal grille being wrenched back. Dr Jones was now nowhere in sight. Davey and Kate moved nearer to Elinor and Tom. They might stand a chance if it was just Monckton on his own, but he appeared to have brought reinforcements. Blackness was seeping from the crack between the lift's wide double doors, pouring through the gap at the bottom, spreading and pooling like Indian ink all across the floor. They had to find somewhere to hide.

# 15

Three floors above, the shadowy galleries seemed deserted, but Derek was not taking any chances. He locked all the doors behind him and retreated to the comparative normality of the foyer and shop area.

He took his cap off and sat behind the desk, slowly wiping the sweat from his face, trying to make sense of what he had seen. He was extremely rattled, badly frightened. He had not believed in ghosts before, not until this moment. If someone had told him yesterday, he would have laughed out loud, but he was not laughing now. Black shadows, they could be a trick of the light, but what he had seen just now? Subsequent to that? He shook his head, wiping his face again, trying to control his shivering.

He would never tell anyone, because no one would believe him, but another night like this and he would seriously consider handing in his notice. It had started in *Seventeenth Century*, right next to *Weaponry*. So real he thought that a member of the public had got themselves locked in. Then he looked again. He twisted his sweat-soaked handkerchief. A highwayman was standing there. Large as life. Next a woman appeared, gliding out of *Domestic*. As if that weren't enough, in the next gallery, one of the figures actually came to life! Walking right out of the tableaux arrangement in *Nineteenth Century/Early Twentieth Century – Costume, Toys and Household Goods*!

'Do you think he saw us?' Elizabeth asked as she joined Jack and Polly. Her grey eyes lit with just a touch of mischief.

'From the look of him, I would say very likely.' Jack Cade's dark eyes danced and a quick smile softened his hawk-like features. Even in these grave circumstances, ghosts found a good haunting hard to resist. 'I would not have marked him as a sensitive, but then you can never tell.'

'Have the Sentinels gone?' Polly looked round carefully, refusing to share their amusement. 'Be serious, Jack. And you, Elizabeth. This is no time for mirth. We have work to do.'

Jack lost his smile and threw back his head, his long black curly hair spilling over his shoulders, his fine nostrils flaring. Sentinel presence was unmistakable. Graveyard mould clung to them. They carried with them the musty, cold earth stench of stone vaults and underground burial.

'They have gone from here. I can only smell a mere trace. We're safe – for the moment.'

'That's as maybe.' Polly's small mouth compressed in a thin line. 'But we are not here to consider our own safety. What about Davey and Kate? And Elinor and Tom? They may be in danger. We were sent here to help them.'

'We know that, Polly,' Elizabeth replied sharply, stung by Polly's scolding. She had helped Davey at Christmas, against the Lady, and considered him to be in her special care.

'We need to keep our wits about us then.' The older woman's black eyes still showed disapproval. 'This is no jaunt. What use would we be to them if Prior Robert and his cohorts suck out our spirits and leave us for wraiths? Without us the children would be in even greater peril. You know what they do to the living. Take the light from their eyes, the life from their bodies and enslave their souls—'

'Polly is right.' Jack frowned. 'They are most formidable foes. We must proceed with caution. We cannot win in face-to-face combat. There are other factors to consider—'

'Such as?' Elizabeth questioned.

Jack did not reply at once. He looked about him. As he did so, the modern museum began to fade. Mushroom emulsion was replaced by dark wood panelling and shadowy faces appeared in the gallery, looking down on dock, witness stand, jury box and, at the far end, the Judge's high bench.

'This building has a long and hideous history,' he said at last, keeping his voice low. 'I, of all people, should know. I stood in this room before the Judge himself. I was kept in the dungeons below. I took my last walk as an earthly man out on to Fetter Lane and from there to the Market Place . . .'

He paused again, pulling at the scarf round his neck as if to ease pain remembered from long ago.

'So?' Elizabeth's eyebrows rose in question. 'We are not here to reminisce.'

'I know that.' He collected himself. 'There may be other crews here, that is all.' His dark expressive eyes showed a new gleam, a mixture of hope and excitement. 'Come, let us waste no more time.'

Steel shutters and locked doors cannot bar a ghost's way. Jack, Elizabeth and Polly glided through steel and wood, stone and concrete, following the Sentinel reek down to the lower basement.

Darkness poured like soot from the lift. Finally the metal doors clanged open and out stepped Monckton. He held the Judge's staff, but nothing else. No sign of the relic . . .

Davey risked a look through the shelves where they were hiding. Maybe he had been wrong. Mixed relief and disappointment flooded through him. Maybe he had already taken the skull somewhere else. Davey was not wrong. What he saw next had him cowering back. Behind Monckton stood another figure. Monckton was tall but this person was much, much bigger. Prior Robert, Chief of the Sentinels, practically dwarfed him as he stepped forward, his monk's robes billowing blackness, a deep cowl hiding his face. He held the skull clutched in his skeletal hands. He checked his step and glanced round.

Davey glimpsed green from sockets set deep in his seamed gaunt face. The creature stood, teeth bared, scenting the air . . .

Davey moved backwards, pushing the others right to the end of the racks. There he was suddenly overcome by fresh panic. He could see now what Dr Jones meant about the shelving. It moved backwards and forwards on grooves set into the floor. One spin of the outer wheel would crush them to death.

He need not have worried, their hiding place stayed undiscovered. The Sentinels turned the other way, forming up in ranks behind Monckton and their leader. Heads bowed, skeletal fingers tucked inside the sleeves of their rotting habits, they moved forward in solemn procession, just like the monks they once were.

'What are we going to do now?' Tom whispered.

'I don't know . . .' Davey shook his head. 'How about if we follow them?'

'I don't think we ought to do that.' Kate looked dubious. 'I think we ought to wait for Jack and his crew. The Fiddler said they would be here to help.'

'Maybe. But what if they're not?' Davey frowned. 'There's no sign of them yet.'

'Perhaps we should go and get Dr Jones,' Elinor suggested.

'And tell her what?' her brother scoffed. 'Time it takes us to explain, the relic will have gone again. She probably won't believe us anyway.' He screwed a finger into his head. 'Think we're crazy. I think we should follow them. I'm with Davey.'

'I think we should stay here—' Elinor started to say.

'You would,' her brother sneered.

'No.' Kate shook her head. 'We have to stick together.' She turned to Elinor. 'If one goes, we all go.'

'Oh, OK.' Elinor gave in. She did not want to be left down here on her own.

'Right.' Tom signalled Davey forward. 'Let's go.'

Davey moved out cautiously. The two girls went next, with Tom bringing up the rear. As they passed the treatment tanks, Tom picked up two big bottles and stowed them in the wide inside pockets of his jacket. He didn't know how the chemical contents would work on Sentinels, but they might just even up the odds.

The procession, led by Prior Robert and Monckton, had already disappeared by the time the children emerged. Davey advanced warily, keeping his eyes wide. There was no sign of Dr Jones. The whole area was changing. The presence of Prior Robert and Sentinels in such numbers was making the whole world unstable. The shelves, the machinery, all evidence of the twentieth century was disappearing. The dry concrete floor of the narrow passage was turning to straw-strewn slimy broken stone sloping down to a central clotted gutter. The walls on either side were rough red brick blackened by smoke from flickering torches. It was as though one world overlay another, with the one underneath growing clearer, getting stronger. A noisome disgusting stink of human filth replaced the sweetish vaguely chemical smell of the modern basement.

As they went on, groans and cries and the clinking of chains told them that the cells on either side were occupied. Thick studded doors were set at intervals along both walls. They fought down the temptation to look in through the small barred windows. Jack Cade had said that in this world, they were as phantoms: most of the ghosts could not see them. They crept past, cringing down, making no sound, praying that the highwayman was right.

The room at the end was empty of prisoners. It looked like a stable divided into wooden stalls, but it was still part of the gaol. Fetters and manacles hung from heavy chains fixed by thick rings to the bulging stone walls. The wooden dividers offered a place to hide. At Davey's signal, they split into two. Davey and Kate taking the right-hand side. Tom and Elinor going to the left.

The Sentinels, hooded and robed, like the corrupted monks they were, stood grouped in a horseshoe at the far end. They seemed to be conducting some kind of ceremony. All their heads were bent in some vile parody of prayer. Fat white candles sputtered in front of a makeshift altar. Chanting filled the air, but it had none of the harmony and beauty of monastic voices joined together. The words were harsh and grating, the sound disturbingly discordant. This was a litany of evil.

Prior Robert stepped forward, tall and terrifying in the

flickering candlelight. Monckton stepped back, head bowed. The children watched paralysed, transfixed. They knew instinctively that to approach, to challenge, would be suicide. They tucked themselves away and stayed motionless, keeping the stillness of the hunted. The slightest movement, the smallest sound, could give them away.

Monckton and his master seemed too absorbed by the ritual to sense interlopers. Sentinels glided from one place to another. Monckton stood head bowed, sidelined. Prior Robert was standing in front of the altar, master of the ceremony. As the chanting increased in intensity, rising towards a climax, he took the skull, lifting it upwards. As he did so, Davey bit his tongue to prevent himself crying out. The screaming in his head was even louder than before, but it struck a new note. Before it had been angry, indignant about being moved at all. Now it had a desperate quality, as if pleading with him to do something. But what? Davey sank down to his knees, head bent in despair. All they could do was watch and hide, hide and watch, as the sacred relics were ritually desecrated and the ceremony rose to its height.

'What are they doing?' Kate whispered. 'What's going to happen?'

Davey shook his head. He had no idea, but it had to be bad. No one went to this much trouble for nothing. It would be bad for the ghosts and for the living. It would mean turmoil in both cities, living and dead.

Kate asked no more questions. They all watched, eyes wide and unblinking. The wall behind the stone slab altar was crumbling, falling in chunks of spongy, rotting masonry. The space revealed was narrow; like a stone coffin. The mummified body of the Judge lay behind the wall. The corpse was wrapped in a rotted shroud, hands folded on chest, neck awry, head set at the angle of a man hanged to death. Then the wasted limbs began to stir, as if from long sleep, and the eyes began to open . . .

The purpose of the ceremony became clear. It was to reanimate a corpse long dead, bring it back to life. But why? What would be the point of going through the world as a rotting corpse? Kate stared on, her mind fighting all the time, trying to shut out what she saw with her eyes.

The wasted corpse was beginning to plump up, take on flesh. At the same time Monckton began to fade. He let out a cry of agony, finally understanding what was about to happen to him. He had been betrayed. These creatures had promised him the knowledge to gain life eternal; but it was *his* life draining away. He was being sacrificed so the Judge could live again. As Monckton staggered sideways, two Sentinels glided forward to hold him upright. The tone of the chanting changed, taking the ceremony to another level. Prior Robert turned, his eyes gleaming green and deadly, his teeth bared in a death's head grin of triumph.

Kate could stand it no longer. She let out a low moan, a

whimper of horror. Prior Robert heard that. Alerted to at least one other living human presence, the green gleam increased to a beam of sickly phosphorescence, igniting the eyes of his cohorts. Prior Robert flung Monckton aside. The man crumpled down, of no more use to him. He signalled his Sentinels to form up behind him. The Ceremony of Possession could work for all, binding any living being to those already dead.

# 16

The Ceremony of Possession cannot work on ghosts. Jack knew that. He also knew the deadly danger the Ceremony posed to the living, the Fiddler had told him, but he could not take on the Sentinels, not with just three in his crew.

They were not alone, however. The place was thick with those who had suffered here and Jack was one of their own. He had spent his last night as a living man inside these walls. All through the basement his crew swelled as ghosts rallied to his call. Men, women and children, tried and condemned, joined the warders and guards who also haunted the place. Usually they squabbled and fought, but this was enough to make them bury their differences. They were all united by their hatred of the Judge.

Jack just hoped they were not too late. The chanting at the far end of the passage acted as a beacon, guiding them to the place. It rose to a crescendo, fierce and hypnotic, so loud and penetrating that he wanted to stop his ears. Then Jack broke into a run, waving his ghostly forces forward. Worse, far worse than the chanting, was the silence that followed it.

'Get back! Get back!' Tom put himself in front of the others, and turned to face the tidal wave of blackness flowing towards them.

'What are you going to do?' Davey's voice was a hoarse whisper. He could see no way out of this. There was no sign yet of the help promised by the Blind Fiddler. They were doomed.

'Here. Cop hold of one of these.' Tom took the big brown bottles from his inside pockets and handed one to his cousin.

'What will it do?' Davey looked at the label, at the black 'X' meaning 'toxic chemical'.

'I don't know. Let's see, shall we?' Tom braced himself, ready to throw.

The bottle exploded right in the middle of the first rank. Fragments of glass showered everywhere as the contents fountained upwards, splattering the leading Sentinels, including Prior Robert. He let out a roar. His hideous face distorted into a raging snarl as the liquid splashed over him, coating him and the other Sentinels with a dripping white substance.

'What is it?' Davey hissed.

'Polyethylene glycol. They use it for preserving wood and stuff.'

'What is it doing to them?'

'Dunno,' Tom shrugged. 'But they don't like it, do they?'

The Sentinels were squirming, writhing away from the chemical pool spreading across the floor. The Prior's face showed the same horror and distaste, but his eyes glowed with command. From his mouth came guttural sounds. He held his skeletal arms high, calming the uproar.

'He's trying to rally them. Time to lob yours. Wait . . . Wait . . .' Tom waited for the right moment. He wanted them bunched closely, not all spread out. 'Now!'

Davey did as he was told. The second attack was even more deadly than the first. They clearly had not been expecting it. The bottle hit Prior Robert full in the face. He fell backwards, the glass container smashing on the floor at his feet. The contents splashed out, catching others, blotching their black robes, but already the Sentinels were dispersing, spreading in all directions.

'We've got them on the run!' Tom let out a shout of triumph.

But where were they going to run to? It wasn't over yet. They might have been scattered by the surprise attack, and some were crippled, affected by the chemicals, but none had been destroyed. They were coming back, forming up into a group again. Davey's heart sank. They had no more ammunition. He looked to Tom who shrugged, palms out.

'Time to get out.'

Tom took a step backwards, and then another. They were in full view of the Sentinels, but the black horde made no move to attack, or even advance towards them. In fact, they were retreating, drawing together for their own protection. Davey pulled Tom's sleeve and pointed. The areas behind and to the side were filled with ghostly figures. Men, women and children were swarming all around. Some were barefoot and in rags, others wore faded tattered clothing, but they all carried a weapon of some kind: stave, plank or chain. In front, sword in hand, came Jack Cade.

'What do you do here, Jack Cade?' Prior Robert's voice had the deep harsh hiss of one unused to speech. His words were hard to distinguish, but their threat and menace were unmistakable. 'This is not your haunting ground. Be warned. All of you.' He extended a wasted arm from his mildewed sleeve, sweeping his bony finger in an arc to take in the rest of the crowd. 'Leave now or face the gravest consequences. You meddle in matters that are none of your concern.'

'Oh, do we?' Jack Cade's eyes narrowed to slits of contempt. 'We know what you seek to do here. To bring the dead alive. It is forbidden.' He eyed the Sentinels, and raised his voice, addressing them all. 'Inform the Judge, your master, that we defy him and his evil purposes. We tire of his tyranny.' Muttered agreement rippled from the ghosts around him, spreading outwards, rising to a muffled roar of assent. 'You may tell him that from me, Jack Cade,' he added, his dark eyes glittering defiance, white teeth showing in a ferocious grin. 'That is, if any of you escape from this place.'

He held his sword high and let it fall. On his command, the ghost crews surged forward.

'Go! Flee!' he shouted to Davey and the others as he

214

passed them. 'You will find Elizabeth and Polly waiting. This is no place for the living.'

He let out a final bloodcurdling yell and the two ghost forces clashed together.

Tom, Kate and Elinor ran back, passing through the surging ghost hordes unnoticed and unmolested. It was as if the ghosts did not see them, as if they were not really there. They turned one corner, then another and the world around them began to shimmer and shiver. The rough brick walls on either side were reverting to painted plaster, the slippery stones beneath their feet becoming grey scuffed concrete. They rounded a final corner and found themselves in the basement as they had first seen it. The lift stood open, as Monckton had left it. Engines hummed, the iron staircase spiralled up to the floor above.

'What is happening down there?' Elizabeth's grey eyes sparked with excitement. She longed to be in the fighting and resented being told to stay here and wait.

'They are fighting the Sentinels. It's turning into a great big battle.' Tom's eyes shone too, as he told her the news. 'Jack's lot are giving them a real pasting—'

'Hold your celebration. They might win now but what is to come?' Polly's eyes were wide with fear. 'The Judge will not like it.' Her hands twisted together in her long apron. 'What if he issues a Declaration? What if we have started a war we cannot win?'

'We gave them something to think about first, though,'

Tom went on, Elizabeth hanging on every word. Polly might as well have been talking to herself. 'We showed them something. Didn't we, Davey? Davey?'

He looked round for his cousin, and then at Kate and Elinor. In their flight, none of them had noticed that Davey was not with them.

They went back the way they had just come, but all they found was a long concrete corridor lit by strips of neon. They listened carefully, straining to hear the noise of battle, but the only sound was the background hum of modern machinery. They were back in their own world and Davey was nowhere to be seen.

## 17

Davey cried out, trying to call the others back, but they were already making a head-long dash for safety. He could not blame them, but in their panic they had forgotten something of the utmost importance. The skull. The relic. The reason they were here in the first place. It was still lying on the makeshift altar. Something told him that it must not be left there.

He threw himself in the direction of the general mêlée, dodging swords and staves and flailing arms. The ghostly weapons passed right through him, they had no power to harm him, but they could certainly inflict damage on each other. All around, remnants of Sentinels, torn to rags of black, littered the ground. Caught by a blow from Prior Robert's staff, a ghost let out a ghastly screech and his form faded to smoke, disappearing right before Davey's eyes. It was hard to tell which way the battle was going, but it seemed to Davey that the Sentinels were retreating. Jack and his army were getting the best of the fighting.

Davey struggled through the confusion, making for the rough altar. He stood in front of it, looking round warily, searching for signs of Monckton. At this moment, human enemies worried him more than ghosts. The dark polished skull was still there, set out on the low stone slab. The relic had been set around with strange signs and little dishes bearing offerings, dried and powdered substances, some of them smouldering and smoking. Davey wrinkled his nose. The scent coming up from them was pungent and disgusting.

Davey sensed a movement, small and slight, to his right. Something creeping, white and glistening. His eyes widened with horror. The magic was still working! The Judge's mortal remains were still animate! Thin tendril hands were creeping out towards him. They were coming out of the wall!

The twisted blackthorn staff lay against the side of the altar where Monckton had left it. Without even thinking, Davey picked it up and lashed out at the white crawling things. The thin skin punctured, ripping and splitting like rubber gloves. The thing gave out a mewling howl and the crippled hands pulled back, foul yellow liquid spurting from the cracks. Davey dodged to avoid getting splashed and then leapt forward to snatch the relic, parcelling up the precious cargo in his coat.

He sped away, avoiding the ghost battle still going on all around him. He ran on and on, looking behind him every now and then, to make sure that he was not being followed.

Once out of the immediate area, he found to his intense relief that the world around him had changed again. He was surrounded by the reassuring hum of high-tech machinery. Safety notices curled on the walls. Thick

218

aluminium trunking curved above his head. He checked his bundle, feeling for the bulge of the skull, wanting to make sure it had not stayed in the world that he had just left. It was still there.

He gave a quick prayer of thanks and looked around him, trying to work out where he was now. He had stumbled into an area unfamiliar to him. Some kind of storage place. He was in a narrow kind of alley between tall racks of shelving stretching away on either side. Davey leaned back against the smooth grey plastic-coated surface of the roller racking, resting his arm against one of the three-pronged wheels that shuttled the shelves backwards and forwards. He stood for a moment, eyes closed, waiting for his heart to stop thumping and for his breathing to return to normal. At least he was back in the twentieth century.

A hoarse voice above him gasped, 'I'll take that.'

Davey's eyes snapped open to see the tall figure of Dr Monckton standing over him. The man was pale and drawn, drained by his ordeal, but his face was grim and determined. He wanted the skull and would do anything to get it. His fingers curled round the Judge's blackthorn staff. He had been betrayed, but he had learnt enough from his spectral friends to know the power the relic contained.

He held the staff above Davey and reached with his other hand to wrench the bundle away from the boy. Davey clutched the bunched coat tighter, struggling and kicking out, but, even in his present weakened state, the man was far too strong for him. He pulled the bundle from him, and brought the stick down heavily, aiming for Davey's head. Davey dodged out of the way, catching his foot on the raised lip at the base of the roller racking. He lost his balance and fell backwards in between the shelves.

He lay on his back, struggling like a beetle to get himself upright. The shelves stretched above him, about an arm's length apart. He had stumbled into *Anthropology*. A bizarre array of stored objects looked down on him: drums, totems and African masks. He reached out, trying to get a purchase on the shelves on either side. They seemed nearer now, making it harder to move his arms. He lay there struggling, a terrible realisation dawning. At first the movement was so small that it was hard to believe that it was happening, but the shelves on either side were definitely moving, closing together. Davey turned his head from side to side in panic, sweat breaking out all over him, as the shelves came nearer and nearer, pinning his arms to his sides.

He let out a yell, a cry for help, but all the time the wheel kept turning and his shout was met by a cynical laugh from the other side. He tried one last desperate effort to heave himself up, but he was wedged too tightly, the slightest movement was now impossible. He was finding it hard to breathe. His shouts were reduced to painful gasps. If someone didn't come soon, he would be crushed to death.

# 18

'What's going on? I thought I heard—' Mari Jones dashed round the corner and then checked her step. 'Oh, Dr Monckton.' She eyed her colleague suspiciously. 'What are you doing here?'

'I could ask you the same thing.'

'All the security shutters are down for some reason. I've been looking for keys in the maintenance office. The internal phones aren't working either. I had to call out and get the Director to phone Derek from home. But like I said,' she returned her original enquiry, slow and even, 'what are you doing here?'

'I have just returned something. I was closing the roller racking.' He took his hands off the wheel and turned as if to go.

'Wait, just a minute.' The archaeologist stepped forward to stop him and caught her foot on something. 'What's this? It looks like a kid's coat . . .'

She knelt down to investigate, opening the bundle carefully, gasping at the unexpected contents. Her long fingers folded back the material and began to feel for any new breaks or damage to the skull. Monckton looked down at the glossy dark red head bent before him, his eyes wild and flecked with lights of madness. He grasped the

Judge's stave tightly and started to raise it, when a muffled groan came from the shelving beside him.

'What's that?' Mari Jones jumped up and went to the gap in the shelving. 'Davey? What are you doing in there?' She acted quickly and spun the wheel backwards, releasing the boy from the crushing force of tons of pressure on either side and stepped in to help him up. She realised her mistake a fraction too late. The shelves were coming back again.

'Monckton! What are you doing! You're turning it the wrong way!'

She was tall and strong. She braced her arms against the oncoming shelves, holding them apart while Davey scrambled to his feet.

Outside, Monckton laughed, intent on his task. He had threaded the Judge's staff through the wheel to get more purchase.

Suddenly he felt cold breath on his neck and a voice in his ear whispered, 'Unhand it.'

He turned and came face to face with a seventeenth-century highwayman. Monckton blinked, convinced that this was a ghost and could not harm him, but the sword at his throat felt real enough. Monckton stretched to his right, reaching for the Judge's staff, but it was snatched from his grasp. A ghost at Jack's side snapped it in half. Behind him there were others, stretching back, more and still more of them. The motley crew of ghosts spread away into the distance. They must have bested the Sentinels.

Jack Cade grinned as Monckton fled.

The pressure was released. Davey and Dr Jones were suddenly free. Davey stepped out, looking round for Monckton. The skull was still there, wrapped in his coat on the floor, the Judge's staff lay broken in two pieces next to it, but the man had gone. Davey looked up to see Jack Cade smiling at him. He smiled back, nodding his thanks.

'What on earth's going on?'

Mari Jones stepped out from the shelving expecting to see Monckton but there was no sign of him, just Davey staring at a patch of thin air. She completely failed to see Jack although she was looking straight at him. The highwayman faded until there was just a little shimmer where he had been standing.

'What's that?' she pointed to the broken staff.

'I don't know . . .' Davey started. 'Dr Monckton had it. Maybe he snapped it.'

'Hmm,' Mari Jones nodded. Perhaps the archivist had experienced some kind of breakdown. He had been acting very strangely lately. Disappearing for no reason, obsessively poring over those papers, not allowing anyone else even to look at them. And his behaviour just now bordered on the bizarre. 'What about the skull? Is it all right?' She knelt down, gently feeling the smooth cranium. 'Seems to be,' she muttered to herself and then sat back on her heels and looked up at Davey. 'What exactly *has* been going on here?' Her green-brown eyes narrowed on him. 'You know, don't you?'

Davey shook his head, trying to play dumb. He liked Dr Jones, liked her a lot. He did not want to tell her things that were untrue. She was intelligent and astute, she would see through lies in a minute. He owed her more than that, his life, in fact. But how could he explain? It would take too long and she'd *never* believe it. He added a little shrug. Best to say as little as possible.

'Where did you find the skull? How did it come to be inside your coat?'

'I – I just found it. Kind of lying around . . . I put it in my coat to be safe.'

'Why would Dr Monckton want to trap you in the roller racking?'

'I – I don't know . . . Perhaps he didn't see me . . . Perhaps he didn't mean to . . .' Davey's voice cracked slightly as he remembered the crushing force of the shelves coming towards him.

'OK, OK,' she said more gently, mindful of his recent ordeal. It wasn't for him to answer. Anyway, questions could wait, at least until they were out of the basement. She gathered up the relic. 'Let's get this to safety. We can look for explanations afterwards.'

## 19

Derek, the guard, was waiting with the other children by the stairs.

'Dr Jones!' He hurried up to the archaeologist, full of apology. 'I'm terribly sorry. I had no idea you were all down here. Then the Director rang in with your message. Something happened to the systems.' He shook his head. 'They were all down, all frozen. They seem all right now.' His worried face brightened, 'I just heard the lift . . .'

The doors were closed. Monckton had gone.

'It's OK, Derek,' she replied. 'We were down here looking for something and then realised we couldn't get out.'

'Was Dr Monckton with you?' Derek peered past her.

'No.' She clutched the bundle tighter. 'Why do you ask?'

'His car is still in the car park.'

It was no longer there when Derek let them out of the building. Monckton's parking space was empty. Mari Jones had a strong feeling that they would not be seeing Dr Monckton again. She imagined that there would be a letter claiming urgent recall to his university: funding suddenly available for some research project that would no doubt take him abroad.

Dr Jones left her own car where it was. The museum was barely a stone's throw from the cathedral. It would be quicker to walk. She took the relics straight there and left them with the Provost. She was not going to wait for carbon dating confirmation; she was convinced in her own mind that these were the bones of St Wulfric and was not going to waste further time in consultation. It was the museum's duty to look after any human remains that came into its possession. There could be no argument, no discussion. It was her judgement that the museum's duty of care was best executed by giving them into the safe-keeping of the church.

The strange occurrences in the museum could be put down to sudden electrical failure and the erratic behaviour of a visiting academic, but Dr Jones knew there was more to it than that. She was a close observer, all archaeologists were, it came with the territory. Landscapes, buildings, people, all came under the same sharp scrutiny and were subject to the same shrewd interpretation. Take these children. They appeared pale and shaken, as if they had all suffered a bad fright – not just Davey. They flinched at the mention of Monckton, and stayed tense and jumpy until the bones were safely in the hands of the Provost. Then it was as if a huge burden had been lifted from their shoulders.

She drove them home after delivering the relics, taking them out of the city back to their home in the suburbs. Davey sat beside her, the others in the back. On the journey, she questioned them. The rest stayed silent, leaving Davey as spokesman. He tried to answer her truthfully, saying that he'd had a feeling about Monckton, that the man was up to no good, and how the feeling had grown and grown until he knew he had to do something about it, that's when they had gone to her. The archae-ologist listened without interrupting and then nodded as if accepting his explanation. She did not question him further.

Hardly another word was spoken all the rest of the way home. Davey looked over at Mari Jones as she drove, trying to read her face in profile. The sharply-chiselled features and taut jawline gave nothing away but he sensed that she understood about feelings. Perhaps she had them herself.

## 20

The Judge sat in his room, studying *The Book of Possibilities*. He traced the Rules, Laws and Statutes of the Ghost City with a bony forefinger. The long nail, curved and twisted, thick as horn, scored deep lines, marking out *What Was, What Is, and What Is To Be*. The book's writ had been questioned. Nay more. Rules had been broken, laws defied, statutes denied. Such open rebellion would not go unpunished. He turned the thick, wrinkled pages, holding them down with his wounded crippled hand, the quill spluttering as he carefully copied out names and places in his thin crabbed writing.

Hostilities had broken out in Ghost City. His own Sentinels were much depleted. He would issue a Declaration, naming the guilty parties. His plans for Monckton might have failed, but he had other human subjects and other strategies. First he would deal with the lesser crews, then it would be the turn of those led by that thorn in his flesh, that nuisance of a highwayman, that villain Jack Cade. He would be destroyed, and his crew with him, scattered like sand, condemned to drift forever in the desolate chaos of time and space. Woe betide any who tried to help him. They would share the same fate. Be they living, or be they dead.

He finished his copying and sanded the parchment.

## In Declaration . . .

In the gathering darkness the rust-coloured letters glowed blood-red as he blew across them with withered lips.

In newly-refurbished offices, across the square from the Judge's house, Mrs Sylvia Craggs was putting the finishing touches to her Chairperson's address for the next meeting of the Society, that is, the Society for the Investigation of Psychic, Paranormal and Associated Phenomena. Now called SIPPAP for short. It had just been the Society for a hundred years or more. Another of the changes that made her far from happy . . . Still, back to the matter in hand . . .

*I am pleased to report*, she wrote, tapping away on her old-fashioned portable typewriter. She did not hold with these new-fangled wordprocessors – *that the recent outbreak of phenomena has abated for the moment, at least* . . .

The city was quiet. Perhaps too quiet? She stopped typing and went to the window. A psychic and a medium, she had the distinct feeling that something was brewing. This was the lull before the tempest. A psychic storm was about to break over the city. The ghosts were at war . . .

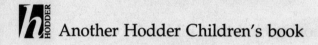 Another Hodder Children's book

**CITY OF SHADOWS**

*Celia Rees*

The start of a compelling trilogy

*All through the city and its suburbs, the past lies behind
the present and ghosts shadow the living. There are
threshold zones, borderlines, and places where the laws of
time and space falter. Strange things can happen, the
barriers between the world's grow thin and it is possible,
just possible, to move from world to another . . .*

It is the summer of his twelfth birthday, and
Davey, his sister Kate, and his twin cousins,
join the hoards of tourists eager to catch a
glimpse of the legendary Underground city
in Davey's hometown. A harmless trip. Just a
bit of fun. But for Davey it is the start of a
nightmare, and a long, terrifying battle with
the dead . . .

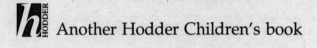

Another Hodder Children's book

**THE HOST RIDES OUT**

*Celia Rees*

The final part in a compelling trilogy

*All through the city and its suburbs, the past lies behind the present and ghosts shadow the living. There are threshold zones, borderlines, and places where the laws of time and space falter. Strange things can happen, the barriers between the world's grow thin and it is possible, just possible, to move from world to another . . .*

Paranormal activity is causing chaos for all who live and work in the city, and Davey is more alert than his sister and cousins to voices from the past. Will the ghosthunter – brought in to investigate, uncover the root of the problem, or is his very presence a trigger for evil spirits to make themselves known . . .? And now Davey must be more on his guard than ever. When Midsummer comes round again, his icily dangerous nemesis, the Lady, will stop at nothing to banish him to a life in hell . . .